"What's the Matter?"
He Demanded. . . .

"Adam," Belinda stammered unhappily, "please try to understand . . . it's very hard for me, too."

"Is it, darling?" His anger was instantly gone and he touched her cheek with his fingertips in a tender gesture. "I love you so much, and I want to think that you love me in return."

Belinda's heart was thudding painfully and her throat felt tight with emotion. Adam, as if suddenly doubtful, said urgently, "You do love me, darling, don't you? Say you do!"

It was so easy to say it. Madness, of course, but so easy! "I love you, Adam," she murmured huskily. "I love you very deeply." In all this tangled web of deceit, that was the one great shining truth.

NANCY JOHN
is an unashamed romantic, deeply in love with her husband of more than thirty years. She lives in Sussex, England, where long walks through the countryside provide the inspiration for the novels that have brought her a worldwide following.

Dear Reader:

I'd like to take this opportunity to thank you for all your support and encouragement of Silhouette Romances.

Many of you write in regularly, telling us what you like best about Silhouette, which authors are your favorites. This is a tremendous help to us as we strive to publish the best contemporary romances possible.

All the romances from Silhouette Books are for you, so enjoy this book and the many stories to come. I hope you'll continue to share your thoughts with us, and invite you to write to us at the address below:

Karen Solem
Editor-in-Chief
Silhouette Books
P.O. Box 769
New York, N.Y. 10019

NANCY JOHN
Make-Believe Bride

Silhouette Romance

Published by Silhouette Books New York

America's Publisher of Contemporary Romance

SILHOUETTE BOOKS, a Simon & Schuster Division of
GULF & WESTERN CORPORATION
1230 Avenue of the Americas, New York, N.Y. 10020

Copyright © 1982 by Nancy John

Distributed by Pocket Books

ISBN: 0-671-57192-3

First Silhouette Books printing December, 1982

10 9 8 7 6 5 4 3 2 1

Map by Ray Lundgren

SILHOUETTE, SILHOUETTE ROMANCE and colophon are
registered trademarks of Simon & Schuster.

America's Publisher of Contemporary Romance

Printed in the U.S.A.

ENGLAND
AND
WALES

SCOTLAND

Glasgow
Edinburgh

NORTH SEA

IRELAND

IRISH SEA

York
Leeds
Manchester
Anglesey
Liverpool
Chester

ENGLAND

CARDIGAN
BAY

WALES

Birmingham

Llanelli
Cardiff

LONDON
★

Bristol
Bath

STRAIT OF DOVER

Bridport
Dorchester

ENGLISH CHANNEL

N
W·E
S

FRANCE

Chapter One

Rosehill Street could rightly claim to lie within the exclusive boundaries of Chelsea, but it had come down in the world from its former elegance. These days its tall nineteenth-century houses were all divided up into studio flats and small apartments. With inexpensive living accommodations in London so scarce, Belinda Vaughn had jumped at the chance of taking over the lease of the attic floor of 16 Rosehill Street from the girl who had been her predecessor at the Piccadilly offices of Orbital Travel.

Cradling in her arms a large brown paper bag of fruit and groceries from the neighborhood supermarket, Belinda ran up the three flights of stairs and dumped her purchases on the kitchen table with a sigh of relief.

"I'm home, Barbie!" she called through to her twin sister above the laughter of a TV comedy show.

"I bought lamb chops for supper; I thought we'd have them with a tossed salad. Okay?"

Barbara appeared in the doorway of the living room. "You didn't think to buy a bottle of wine, too, I suppose? I could certainly use a drink."

"Sorry, it never occurred to me. But there's plenty of soda in the fridge."

"Oh, well, I guess I'll have to make do with that."

Strangers had always been astonished to see the two sisters side by side, for in height and physical appearance they were identical. Slender and delicately boned, they each possessed a luxuriant mass of wavy auburn hair and beautiful green-gold eyes set widely apart in a face that was perfectly oval-shaped. When they were children, growing up in a small town in the Catskills, it had been a long-standing joke that no one but their parents could tell the Vaughn twins apart. Sometimes, as a prank, they had deliberately bewildered their teachers and friends by pretending to be each other. Now that they led entirely separate lives, though, there were subtle differences in the two girls' appearance—as at the present moment. Belinda, after her rush-hour scramble across London by bus on this wet January evening, looked, and felt, distinctly shop-soiled compared with her sleekly groomed, ten-minutes-older sister. Furthermore, Barbara was wearing a fabulous, figure-hugging dress in black jersey silk, elaborately trimmed with colored beads, that Belinda hadn't seen before.

"You're very dressed up for an evening at home," she commented, fetching two cans of cola. "Is it new?"

Barbara smiled complacently as she twirled around expertly to display the dress. "I found it in a super little boutique on Bond Street this morning. Like it?"

"Sure I do! But it must have cost a fortune."

"What's money?"

Belinda laughed ruefully. "It's easy for you to say that, Barbie, with a well-off husband to foot your bills. Me, I'm just a poor working girl struggling to make ends meet in this expensive city. If you're planning to keep that dress on," she warned, "you'd better slip on an apron while we cook supper."

Barbara's green-gold eyes took on a wary expression. "Oh, about that . . . I won't be in this evening, after all."

"But you promised!" Belinda couldn't suppress her disappointment. "We agreed that as we'd ended up seeing so little of each other during your trip to London, you'd stay home tonight so we could have a really good talk."

Barbara took a long drink of soda before replying. "I know I did, Bel, but some things have to take priority over a cozy supper at home with one's sister."

"For instance?" asked Belinda suspiciously.

"Can't you figure it out?"

"That Nigel Dixon, I guess you mean?"

"Who else?" said Barbara on a quick bubble of laughter. "He called this morning to suggest taking me to a new nightspot he's discovered in Mayfair. Hence the dress!"

Belinda gave her a reproachful look. "What would Adam say if he knew you'd been dating another man during your stay in London?"

"Adam won't find out, will he, Bel? Not unless *you* tell him!"

Belinda felt a surge of bitterness. "I just don't know how you can cheat on your husband like this, Barbara. Adam is such a wonderful man, and—"

"I might have guessed that you'd stand up for him, but you just can't imagine how deadly dull my life's been since we got married. It's only been ten months, do you realize, and it seems more like ten

9

years. A ten-year jail sentence!" At Belinda's gasp of protest, she rushed on, "Okay, okay, Adam is as sexy as they come, I admit that. If I was just looking for a man to have an affair with he'd be the one I'd choose. There's no question about it. But however fantastic that side of my marriage may be, it doesn't make up for the long days of boredom I have to endure. Have you any idea what it's like to be stuck in the back of beyond of wildest Wales, tied to a man who considers his awful stud farm the most important thing in the world, and expects his poor wife to join in and share his enthusiasm?"

"But you love horses!" Belinda exclaimed. "When we were kids we used to spend every minute we could playing around Uncle Hiram's stables."

"That was a long time ago," pointed out Barbara dryly. "I've developed a few other interests since those days!"

Dismayed by her sister's tone, Belinda argued fiercely, "But surely when you're in love with a man, Barbie, you love him for what he is and what he does . . . everything about him."

Barbara gurgled in ironic amusement. "You're a hopeless romantic, Bel, that's your trouble. I'll tell you this for free . . . you can thank your lucky stars that Adam Lloyd switched his attention to me. I know you were pretty gone on him, weren't you? But just think, Bel! If Adam had proposed to you instead of to me, you'd have been landed in the ghastly situation that I'm in now."

A fierce thrust of pain stabbed at Belinda's heart. For a few delirious days last winter she had foolishly allowed herself to believe that the attractive Welshman she'd met while on a ski holiday in Switzerland was on the point of asking her to marry him. But then, as so often with the men she'd dated, Adam Lloyd had apparently come to realize that whatever had first attracted him to Belinda Vaughn existed in double strength in her twin sister. As a fashion model, Barbara possessed superb poise and self-confidence, impeccable grooming and an altogether mysterious extra something that gave her terrific appeal. Suddenly Belinda had found herself dropped flat, with Adam paying all his attention to Barbara instead. Even before the brief holiday came to an end their wedding plans were fixed.

Winning that ski vacation for two at the luxury resort in Switzerland had seemed like a fantastic stroke of luck to Belinda. Each year the Orbital Travel organization offered such a prize for the best promotional suggestion made by a member of its worldwide staff during the previous twelve months. When it was announced that Belinda Vaughn of the New York corporate headquarters had won for her Meet Your Favorite Author vacation-package idea she had been the envy of all her colleagues. She came in for a lot of teasing about which lucky man she'd choose as her companion. But there was no extra-special man in Belinda's life. And in any case, she'd have felt mean not to offer to share her good fortune with her twin, especially as Barbara was in one of her emotional troughs at the time. Not only had she just split with her latest boyfriend, but at twenty-three years old she'd stopped getting so many bookings for the sort of swinging young look that was her modeling specialty. In consequence, she was feeling depressed about her whole future—personal and professional.

In any event, even before Belinda suggested it, her sister took it for granted that she'd be going along, too.

"I could just do with a couple of weeks at a really super hotel," she'd sighed ecstatically. "Imagine it—being pampered and waited on hand and foot."

The luxury aspect of the vacation had appealed to Belinda, too, but she didn't intend to miss out on the splendid facilities for winter sports. So, early on their first morning at the Hotel Edelweiss, she left Barbara still in bed and ventured out alone. While waiting to get her equipment she fell into conversation with a tall, dark-haired Welshman who introduced himself as Adam Lloyd. On learning that she was a beginner he gave her some individual lessons on the beginners' slope. Belinda felt rather guilty about keeping someone who was so obviously an expert from the more challenging runs, but Adam brushed her apologies aside with a friendly grin. They returned to the hotel for lunch together and—truth to tell—Belinda felt rather relieved that Barbara was nowhere to be seen. In the afternoon she and Adam tried ice-skating and Belinda found to her delight that in this sport she was nearly as expert as he was.

When they parted at the end of the afternoon Adam asked Belinda what she'd like to do later on.

"I'm not sure about this evening," she said doubtfully. "It depends on what my sister wants to do."

"Perhaps she could join us," Adam suggested pleasantly.

But Belinda couldn't imagine Barbara making a quiet third. It would be instinctive to her to try and captivate this highly attractive man, with whom Belinda knew already that she could so very easily fall in love. "No . . . no, I don't think I'd better make any plans," she said.

Adam looked gratifyingly disappointed. "Let's leave it open, shall we? I'll keep an eye out for you, and if we do meet up that will be great."

"Okay. Thanks."

Upstairs in their luxury bedroom Belinda was delighted to discover that Barbara had arranged a date for that evening. It seemed that she'd met a man in the lounge that morning and they'd driven to the nearby town for lunch, which explained why

Belinda hadn't been able to find her sister around anywhere. This evening he was planning to take her to a casino. He was a German, named Carl Winthur, a business executive in some branch of electronics, and it appeared that he was very wealthy. Barbara chattered about him vivaciously, seeming uninterested in Belinda's plans. "I guess that I'll be seeing a lot of Carl while we're here, but I bet you'll meet up with someone to keep you company."

So Belinda was free to spend the evening with Adam after all, and it was wonderful. They had dinner together and danced, and afterward they strolled outside in the moonlight, holding hands. Belinda had never before felt so much on the same wavelength with any man and the lovely evening seemed all too short. When they finally parted Adam drew her into his arms to kiss her good night. It wasn't a pushy, demanding kiss, which she always resented on a first date, but light and friendly. Even so, Belinda was conscious of his stirring desire and she felt a thrill of sensuous excitement that stayed with her until she finally fell asleep.

The following four days were sheer bliss for Belinda. Unbelievably, Adam seemed to want to spend all his time with her, and before long she knew that she had fallen helplessly in love with him. She would catch herself secretly studying his profile through her silky auburn lashes while he patiently continued to teach her to ski, admiring his firm straight nose and determined jawline. His long lean face was serious while he concentrated, then his dark eyes would suddenly dance with laughter when she goofed. She thrilled at his slightest touch, on the ski slopes when he corrected her stance, or on the dance floor in the evenings, when he held her close against his lean, sinewy body.

She was greedy to learn all there was to know about him and Adam talked readily. He was the owner of a horse farm in a mountain valley in central Wales, where he bred Welsh ponies, which were now in great demand for riding and pony-trekking.

"I was lucky," he told Belinda. "I'd always wanted to work with horses, and after university I spent three years learning the ropes with a leading racehorse trainer. When he retired I had the chance to buy a superb stallion named Apollo, and at the same time this valley called Glyn-y-Fflur came onto the market. I'd already seen it and knew that it was an ideal site for a stud farm. So I scraped together the necessary cash with the money my parents had left me and a bank loan and whatever. That was six years ago, when I was twenty-five. My luck held and I've never looked back."

"It sounds to me," Belinda said, smiling, "more like a case of seizing your opportunities, rather than luck. What a lovely name . . . Glyn-y-Fflur. What does it mean in English?"

"The Valley of Flowers—and it really is that, especially in springtime, when the bluebells and primroses are out in the woods and the meadows are ablaze with buttercups and moon daisies."

"It sounds beautiful," she breathed.

"It is," Adam confirmed. "I'm prejudiced, of course, but to me it's the most beautiful place on earth. I have to leave it now and then, on business trips to various parts of the world. And I always manage to squeeze in a fortnight's skiing each winter. But every time I return to Glyn-y-Fflur I feel a thrill of pride to think that it's mine."

In turn, Adam asked Belinda about her own background. She explained that their parents had been tragically drowned in a sailing accident when she and Barbie were thirteen years old, and that afterward they had lived with their father's brother and his wife, who had two sons and a daughter of their own, all a bit older than the twins.

"Uncle Hiram is retired now," Belinda said, "but he had a shop in our hometown in the Catskill Mountains that supplied all kinds of camping equipment. As a sideline he always used to keep a few horses to hire out to the vacationers, which was lovely for us."

"So horses have been important in your life, too?" Adam commented interestedly.

"They sure have! I guess you could say that Barbie and I were almost raised in the saddle, because we used to spend a lot of time at the stables even before Mom and Dad died. And I'll tell you this, Uncle Hiram always made us do our full share of the chores . . . grooming and mucking and so on." Belinda didn't think it necessary to add that Barbie had hated that side of it, though she hadn't been allowed to duck out.

After dinner that evening they strolled together as usual across the snow-mantled meadows around the hotel, with bright moonlight casting the long blue shadows of the fir trees. When Adam stopped and took Belinda in his arms his kiss was deep and passionate, flooding her through with warm delight.

At long last he released her and murmured softly against her temple, "You're so beautiful, Belinda. I think I'm in danger of falling in love with you. I always imagined that it might be like this. Suddenly, unexpectedly."

He kissed her again, and as his tongue thrust into her mouth to taste the inner sweetness Belinda gave a gasp of arousal and pressed herself more intimately against him, her own soaring desire matching his. It was as if she was being swept along willy-nilly on a great ocean roller, but she didn't care. She had never felt so ecstatically happy in the whole of her life and she wanted this magical moment to continue for all eternity. While they remained locked in each other's arms, heedless of time passing, the moon slid silently behind one of the mountain peaks and they were enclosed in their own little world of velvet darkness.

When at last they got back to the hotel Belinda was dismayed to see Barbara sitting alone in the foyer, flipping through a magazine and looking very disconsolate. Belinda knew it was too good to be true that she had managed to avoid a meeting between Adam and her sister for so long. With a sinking heart she introduced them.

"Belinda explained to me that you were identical twins," he said, glancing from one to the other in amazement. "But it just doesn't seem possible that any two girls can be so much alike. Both so incredibly beautiful, too!"

Barbara brightened at once and dimpled a smile at him. "When you get to know us better, Adam Lloyd, you'll discover that there are quite a lot of differences between us."

He laughed. "I'll look forward to that."

While Adam went off to order drinks Belinda asked her sister why she had been looking so gloomy when they walked in. Barbara pulled a long face. "It's terrible! Carl had to dash back to Munich because one of his stupid kids has got the measles or something. You'd think his wife would let her husband enjoy his vacation in peace."

This was the first Belinda had heard of Carl's wife and children, but she hid her surprise and inner relief that he was now gone.

Barbara managed to throw off her mood of depression when Adam returned and for the next hour she chatted to him vivaciously, leaving Belinda out of the conversation almost entirely. Later, upstairs in their room, Barbara remarked thoughtfully, "That's quite a man you've found there, Bel. How did you manage it? Don't you find yourself rather out of your depth with someone like him?"

By now it was Belinda who was sunk in a mood of despondency and she felt a cold shiver of fear sneaking down her spine, fear that proved to be well-founded when, next morning, Barbara joined up with them on the ski slopes. As a total beginner she kept claiming Adam's attention, grabbing hold of him laughingly each time she lost her balance on the unaccustomed skis. By that evening Belinda knew that what she had most dreaded was happening right before her eyes, as it had happened in the past.

In the days that followed she found herself the odd one out, and Adam and her sister seemed to spend more and more time alone together. Belinda knew in her heart that there was no chance for her now with Adam Lloyd. Angrily she told herself that if she had one atom of common sense she would show a little encouragement to one of the other unattached men at the hotel who had made their interest in her very apparent. But never before had she fallen so desperately in love and she kept on hoping for a miracle.

On the next-to-last day of the vacation her hope was finally quenched when Barbara told her with shining eyes that she wouldn't be returning to the United States.

"I'm going home to Wales with Adam and we'll be married right away," she said excitedly. "Oh, Bel, I'm so thrilled. He really is a terrific hunk of man!"

Blinking back the tears that stung her eyelids, Belinda summoned up words of congratulations and somehow managed to conceal her wretchedness. The very last day of the vacation was an agony, seeing Barbara and Adam looking so deliriously happy together. Belinda had rehearsed a few sentences of congratulations for Adam, too, and she fervently hoped that she wouldn't give herself away as she delivered them. But Adam barely glanced at her while she was speaking and she guessed that he wanted to forget that there had ever been any kind of intimacy between them.

Flying back to New York with an empty seat beside her, Belinda felt sick with unhappiness. It seemed to her that she never wanted to set eyes on Barbara or Adam ever again; it would be too painful. But as the months went by she felt a growing sense of emptiness. Barbara was her closest relative . . . and as identical twins there had always been a special tug of affinity between them. So when the chance came for Belinda to trade jobs for a year with a girl at Orbital Travel's London branch as part of the firm's scheme for giving their staff international experience, she seized it eagerly.

Belinda had anticipated an invitation to spend weekends at the stud farm in Wales whenever she could manage it and she steeled herself to the prospect of meeting Adam again, this time as her brother-in-law. Instead, though, Barbara landed on her doorstep in Chelsea a few days after her arrival, announcing that she'd come to stay for a vacation.

"Your coming to Britain, Bel, made a good excuse for me to get away from the wilds and back to where there's some life going on," she'd explained with a laugh. In conversation it soon emerged that Barbara had met a "simply gorgeous" man on the train from Wales and she started seeing Nigel Dixon constantly. She did little more than sleep and breakfast at the flat in Chelsea, ignoring Belinda's protests that it was unfair to Adam. Tonight, however, she had agreed to stay home, since it was her next-to-last evening in London. But now, despite her promise, she had blithely announced that she was having dinner with Nigel Dixon yet again.

"I think it's criminal of you to treat Adam this way!" Belinda exploded bitterly. "You're supposed to be in London to see me and show me around, but instead you've spent nearly all your time with a man you picked up on the train coming here. And then the day after tomorrow you expect to go back to your husband and carry on as if nothing had happened."

"Correction," Barbara drawled lazily. "Actually, I wasn't going to tell you this until the very last minute, because I knew you'd make such a hassle. But now that you've raised the subject, I'd better give it to you straight. Nigel is going on an extended business trip around the Far East—Japan, Hong Kong, Singapore, you name it—and he's asked me to go along with him."

Belinda stared at her sister in horror, hardly able to believe her ears. "But what on earth are you going to tell Adam?"

"Nothing! Nothing at all!" There was a defiant tilt to Barbara's auburn head and an ugly twist to her mouth. "I don't see the point of laying myself open to a lot of reproaches and recriminations. So I'm just going to fade out of his life. It's simplest that way, don't you think? Nigel and I are off tomorrow morning."

Belinda was swept through with rage. "You can't do that! I . . . I won't let you."

"Really?" Barbara shrugged her elegant shoulders. "Exactly how do you intend to stop me? Lock me up in the bedroom and call Adam to come at once? But it wouldn't make the slightest difference if he was here. My mind is made up, Bel, and that's final!"

It was totally outrageous. Belinda wanted to shout and scream at her sister about the trail of misery she so heedlessly left behind her. Barbara had always followed the whim of the moment, grabbing what she wanted with both hands, never pausing to think first. She seemed totally indifferent to the havoc she was causing in the lives of the other people involved.

Belinda felt tempted to point out to her that if she hadn't made a play for Adam in Switzerland he might now be married to a wife who loved him with all her heart. A wife who couldn't imagine anything more wonderful than spending the rest of her life with him.

Often during these past months, when her guard was down, Belinda had found herself dreaming of what might have been if Adam Lloyd had proposed to her instead of to her more glamorous twin sister. Piecing things together from the sparse information in Barbara's infrequent letters and what Adam had told her, she'd formed a mental picture of the stud farm, tucked away in its remote Welsh valley, Glyn-y-Fflur. The Valley of Flowers. There would be lush green meadows, watered by a sparkling river and neatly fenced with white palings, the ancient stone-built house standing a little apart from the stables and sheds and the dwellings of the hired hands. And hemming in the valley on all sides, leaving just a narrow pass giving access to the outer world, were softly rounded hills and the blue-hazed mountains of North Wales beyond. A veritable Shangri-la, it had sounded to her, a heavenly spot for a man and a woman in love.

The image had lain in Belinda's mind like a bittersweet vision, though she had tried hard not to resent and envy her sister's marvelous happiness and good fortune. And now she found that her twin placed no value whatever upon something that she herself would have treasured beyond price. It increased her pain a thousandfold to find that Barbara was contemptuously throwing all this away in exchange for the heady excitement of an affair with Nigel Dixon. It wouldn't last, of course. And when it was over, what then? Another man, and then another, and another . . . ?

Belinda closed her eyes to hold back the pain. She

said huskily, "You've got to face up to Adam and tell him your plans, Barbie; it's only fair. Even if you're quite determined not to go back to him you at least owe him a proper explanation. You'd only need to delay your departure a day or so."

Barbara shook her head stubbornly. "I've told you—I just don't want a lot of hassle. Besides, Nigel's got the flight booked for us and everything. Don't bother making an issue of it, Bel; I'm leaving with him first thing tomorrow morning. Luckily I thought to grab my passport before I left for London. So you see, there's nothing to go back to Wales for. Nigel is positively loaded, so there'll be no problem replacing clothes and things."

"At least call Adam!" Belinda pleaded. "That won't delay you and it wouldn't be quite so dreadful as just disappearing out of his life without any explanation at all."

Barbara's face took on a sulky, mulish expression that Belinda knew well. "If you're so bothered about it, Bel, you'd better call the man yourself and break the sad news."

Belinda gasped in protest. "I couldn't! I mean, imagine how Adam would feel to hear over the phone that his wife had left him."

The slender shoulders were lifted again in a shrug of indifference. "So forget it, Bel! After all, it's really no concern of yours, for heaven's sake." Barbara picked up her handbag and rummaged for a cigarette, then spotted something else and pulled it out. "Hey, here's an idea. This is my return rail ticket for Saturday morning . . . first-class reserved seat. You use it, Bel . . . go and commiserate with Adam about his rotten luck. He'll cough up to pay your fare back to London. It would be a nice break for you, and maybe once you've seen Glyn-y-Fflur you'll understand why I'm getting away from the place."

Belinda shook her head, refusing to take the ticket that her sister held out to her. "That's a ridiculous idea. What could I possibly say to Adam?"

"Say anything you like." Barbara giggled. "You could try telling him what a thoroughly rotten excuse for a human being your sister is and that he's well rid of her. That's what you think, isn't it? But I doubt Adam would believe you, Bel, because he's always been crazy about me." She sighed wearily. "It's just a pity the feeling isn't mutual."

"If you don't love Adam you never should have married him in the first place," said Belinda angrily.

"Oh, we're back to 'love' again! Well, let me tell you, love is just a lot of nonsense. When a guy says he loves you it just means that he wants to go to bed with you. My advice, Bel, is always to keep things on that level and you won't make mistakes."

"Look who's talking!" accused Belinda bitterly. "You made a dreadful mistake over Adam."

"But not," corrected Barbara, "because I was stupid enough to imagine that I was in love with him. We could have had a perfect marriage if only he'd had the sense to do what I wanted and sell that stud farm of his so we could live somewhere civilized. He'd get a lot of money for the place if he put it on the market, you know . . . enough so he wouldn't have to work again for the rest of his life. It seems such a terrible waste, all that cash tied up in horse-flesh."

"Adam isn't the playboy type," Belinda threw out. "Surely you could tell that the first moment you met him?"

Barbara shrugged. "I guess I was fooled by the fact that he was staying at a luxury ski resort. I didn't realize that it was a strictly once-a-year indulgence. At other times, though Adam gets around quite a bit, it's horses, horses all the way . . . meeting other breeders, buyers, trainers. When we flew to Spain last summer it was incredibly boring. We stayed at some huge ranch where the only company I had was the owner's stodgy, middle-aged wife, and she couldn't even speak much English. The men were out all day long and didn't get back till dinnertime. And even then they did nothing but talk horses. Just imagine!''

A hot retort sprang to Belinda's lips, but before she could get it out she heard the sound of a car horn from the street below. Barbara went quickly to the window and peered down.

"Good, it's Nigel! I'll have to dash. Don't wait up for me. I'll see you in the morning before you leave for work and say good-bye."

With that Barbara vanished into the bedroom, to reappear in a stylish black suede coat, which also looked like a new acquisition. With a final *"Ciao"* she clattered off down the stairs on her dizzily high heels. In a daze, Belinda heard the front door slam, and moments later the waiting car revved up and drove off. She stood hovering ineffectually in her little kitchen for a long time before at last making an effort to prepare some supper for herself. But she had little appetite and left most of the food on her plate.

When Belinda got home Friday evening she found plenty of evidence of her sister's visit in the form of lots of discarded wrapping paper, an unmade bed and breakfast things left on the kitchen table. Tucked under the butter dish there was an envelope, and scrawled on the outside in Barbara's large handwriting were just two words. *Why not?* Inside the envelope was her rail ticket to Wales.

It was crazy! Belinda grew hot with embarrassment at the mere thought of confronting Adam with the news that his wife had decided to leave him. He might even blame *her,* believing that she must have influenced Barbara in some way. And yet, Adam had to know. If she did nothing about telling him he'd be sure to call tomorrow night, demanding to know why Barbara hadn't returned as expected. She'd have to tell him then. Wouldn't it be better to take the bull by the horns and go and see Adam face to face? That way he couldn't claim that she was trying to dodge the issue. Ridiculously, it mattered to her that Adam Lloyd shouldn't think badly of her.

Belinda spent a wretched evening and went to bed still in a fever of uncertainty about what to do. Precisely when her decision was made she couldn't be sure, but when she woke up the next morning after a restless night of tossing and turning she found that her mind was made up. The train, she knew, left Paddington Station at ten-fifteen. That gave her time to shower, eat what breakfast she could manage and pack a small bag with overnight necessities. By nine-thirty she was aboard a red double-decker bus, sailing through the Saturday streets of London.

But once on the train, as it raced through winter-bare countryside, she could no longer thrust away her apprehensions. Towns and villages flashed past, cattle placidly chewed fodder spread out for them in the frost-rimed fields. And each racing minute she was one mile nearer the confrontation that she dreaded.

What was she going to say to him? What words would she use to help him understand? Were there any excuses she could make for Barbara? Could she lay some of the blame on Adam himself for not appreciating that her twin sister needed more excitement than a quiet life in a remote Welsh valley . . . a life in which horses were the be-all and end-all? But how could she hope to bring conviction to such a charge when she herself could imagine no more wonderful life than being married to Adam—wherever his home was, whatever his occupation?

Belinda had to change from the express to a local train at a place called Llanelli, but the name, when spoken by the conductor, sounded nothing at all like what the spelling suggested. Belinda heard the soft lilt of Welsh voices and listened fascinatedly to the talk around her while she consumed a sandwich and a cup of coffee in the buffet.

Stopping frequently at little stations, the local train wound into a range of mountains . . . the Black Mountains of Wales, she was informed with pride by another passenger. As they progressed, the landscape grew wilder and more remote. The rounded summits were etched sharply against the cold gray-blue of the winter sky, barren above their tree-mantled lower slopes. Often the train rumbled over a rushing stream of sparklingly clear water, and once Belinda spotted a pair of deer leaping agilely from rock to rock toward the protective concealment of a coppice.

It was two hours before Belinda reached her destination, a tiny station with not a town or village in sight. She was the only passenger to alight, and the whole place looked deserted but for the man who sold tickets. It was a relief, when she walked out to the small cobbled courtyard, to find a taxi waiting. Just as she was about to ask the driver if he could take her to Glyn-y-Fflur he jumped out and opened the door for her.

"Good afternoon to you, Mrs. Lloyd."

"Oh, but I'm not . . ." she began in dismay, then hesitated, wondering what to say. How could she explain to this man why, rather than Adam Lloyd's wife, it was her twin sister who had alighted from the train? While she was floundering for words he went on, "You'll be wanting to go straight to the hospital, I'm thinking."

25

"The . . . the hospital?" she stammered.

"Yes, indeed! You won't wish to be delaying before you see your husband."

All thoughts of explanations were swept from Belinda's mind. "What are you saying? Why is Adam at the hospital? Is he ill? Has he had an accident?"

"You don't know, then, Mrs. Lloyd? I thought you must have been informed. Mr. Lloyd was thrown by one of his stallions and got crushed."

Belinda's hands flew to her face in horror. "Is he . . . is he badly hurt?"

"Some men might not have survived," the driver went on, giving her a look of sympathy. "As it is, your husband will be a long time mending, from what I hear."

"When . . . when did this happen?" she asked faintly.

"Yesterday morning, Mrs. Lloyd. He was exercising the—"

"Please, take me to him at once," she interrupted, jumping into the cab.

The taxi swerved out of the station yard and sped along a narrow lane that ran beside a tumbling, boulder-strewn river. But Belinda hardly noticed her surroundings. Her heart was thudding wildly in anticipation of what she might find when she reached the hospital . . . wherever it might be. To ask the driver how far they had to go was out of the question. To reveal such ignorance would be tantamount to admitting that she wasn't the woman he had taken her to be, and it was unthinkable now to risk giving even the smallest hint of Barbara's desertion of her husband before she got a chance to tell Adam himself.

Her mind spun in a whirlpool of anguished thought. How could she contact Barbara to let her know what had happened? Her sister had blithely refused to give any exact information of where her travels with Nigel Dixon would take her, except to say that their first destination was Singapore. Perhaps, thought Belinda, she could cable or phone someone in authority out there who could track down which hotel they were staying at. But would her sister be booked in as Mrs. Lloyd, or as Mrs. Dixon? It all seemed so impossibly difficult.

She became aware that they had reached a town. After crossing an ancient three-arched stone bridge the taxi swept along a wide main street flanked with little gabled houses, a hotel, a garage and some shops. They turned in between tall gateposts, then drove up the short driveway of what had clearly once been a large private mansion. Belinda caught the name on a signboard: PENYSTRAD HOSPITAL.

As she fumbled in her purse for money to pay the driver he said in a tone of surprise, "On the account it will go, Mrs. Lloyd . . . as per usual, isn't it?"

"Oh, right, I wasn't thinking."

To argue the point would arouse his curiosity. Besides, she was in too great a hurry. Nodding her thanks, she ran up the front steps and into the entrance lobby. A girl in a white smock looked up from the reception desk and smiled sympathetically at Belinda.

"Your husband is in Room Twelve, Mrs. Lloyd. That's upstairs, first door on the right along the left-hand corridor. I expect you'll be wanting to go straight up and see him?"

Belinda paused uncertainly. "How . . . how is he?"

"Well, it's best for you to have a word with Sister or Dr. Llewelyn about that. But between you and me, they say he's doing marvelously well, considering. The doctors reckon that he's got the constitution of one of those fine stallions of his."

Belinda hurried up the stairs. Reaching the upper

hall, she glanced around to get her bearings, and the next moment she was hesitating outside the door of Room 12. Now that she was on the very brink of the encounter with Adam she felt like turning tail and fleeing . . . not stopping until she got back to London and her little attic flat in Chelsea.

And where would that leave Adam? He was expecting his wife to return home today, and naturally he would expect her to hasten to his bedside the moment she got news of his accident. What would he think, lying there badly injured, with no explanation of Barbara's absence? Whatever the shock he would feel on hearing of her desertion, it couldn't be worse for him than to be left in doubt about what might have happened to her.

Screwing up her courage, Belinda knocked timidly on the door. A voice called to her to come in, a voice that she recognized with a stab of remembered longing, despite the fact that it lacked Adam's normal firm, resonant tone. Taking a deep breath, she turned the handle and entered the room, which was small and clinically white.

Adam was propped up on a stack of pillows on the narrow hospital bed, his forehead bandaged, his face very pale. But his deep-set, dark eyes lit up at the sight of her. He stretched out his hand in welcome and struggled to raise himself, then fell back again, pain flickering across his lean features.

"Barbie, darling!"

She advanced nervously toward the bed. "But, Adam, I'm not . . . I mean . . ."

"It's been a terrible shock for you, poor love!" He took her hand and gave it a little squeeze, and Belinda felt a flurry of sensual excitement at his touch. "I debated whether to get someone to phone you at Belinda's," he went on, "but it seemed a pity to spoil whatever you two girls had planned for your last evening together. And it wasn't as if there was anything you could do, darling, even if you had come rushing back yesterday. So I just told them to have Thomas meet your train with his taxi and I've been waiting impatiently for you to arrive."

As if in a trance, Belinda allowed Adam to draw her forward so that he could kiss her. A tremor passed through her whole body as their lips connected. She was achingly conscious of the warm, sweet intimacy and she could taste the faint male saltiness of him. She had to resist a mad impulse to curl her arms about his neck and press her cheek against his. A faint moan escaped her as somehow she found the willpower to draw away.

Chapter Two

"Adam . . . what happened?" Belinda stammered, trying to steady her emotions. "All I've been told is that you were thrown by one of the stallions and . . ."

Adam retained his clasp on her hand with eager determination and she couldn't bring herself to wrench away. But where he touched her it felt as if her skin was on fire.

"It was Apollo," he said with a frown. "I've never had any serious problems with him before, and I just can't understand it. I was exercising him along the riverbank and I took him over the footbridge. I know he's always shied a bit just there since the time he threw you at that spot, but I've always been able to coax him before. He was a bit on edge, though, because there was a low-flying plane around, and I suppose the two things coming together were just too much for him." Adam looked at her questioningly. "You never did tell me precisely what happened that day."

Belinda stared at him bewilderedly. This was insanity! Every moment she allowed Adam's misapprehension to continue made it that much more difficult to explain. She opened her mouth to stammer out the truth and something of her reluctance must have conveyed itself to him. With a reassuring little smile he said quickly, "Never mind about that now, darling. We can discuss Apollo later. The important thing is that you're here!" His dark eyes took on a tender, loving expression as he looked at her. "I can't tell you how wonderful it was for me when you walked in through that door and I saw the anxious look on your face. You know, I've been having the craziest thoughts, Barbie. I suppose it was the result of all the sedatives and things they've been pushing into me."

"What do you mean, Adam?" Belinda asked dazedly. "What kind of thoughts?"

His tone was apologetic. "It sounds utterly stupid now. But the truth is, I was dreading that you might not come back to me. It doesn't make any kind of sense, does it? But lying here, I've been thinking about our life together. Things haven't been too good, have they, and I realize that a lot of it must have been my fault. I've been planning how I could make things at Glyn-y-Fflur better for you in future and then I began getting this awful feeling that maybe I'd never have the chance to. I started to feel desperate, stuck here unable to move. I was afraid that I might have lost you forever."

Dear heaven! Was this the moment to tell Adam that his worst fears had been realized? That his wife had indeed walked out on him, quite callously, without even bothering to tell him she was going? Weakened as he was, such news might have a disastrous effect, seriously setting back his chances of recovery. In that agonized moment Belinda made the fateful decision to delay telling Adam of her sister's desertion. For the present he must be allowed to cling to the illusion that *she* was his wife. And that, as a good wife should be, she was very concerned about him.

If only it were true that she was Adam's wife! Belinda closed her eyes against the tormenting thought. Inwardly she raged anew against Barbara for casually throwing away what she herself thought the most precious thing imaginable. Once she had believed that she had won Adam Lloyd's love, only to have it snatched away from her by her sister's superior charms. How was it, she agonized, that life could be so horribly unfair?

With her eyes still closed, Belinda felt Adam lift the hand he was holding, felt his lips lightly brush her fingertips in a loving caress. A tremor of emotion shook her and she became rigidly tense.

"What happened to your ring, darling?" he asked in sudden surprise.

Her green-gold eyes flew open. "My . . . my ring?"

"Your wedding ring. I don't think I've ever seen you without it before."

Belinda flushed scarlet and improvised wildly. "Oh, it was a bit tight, and . . . and . . ."

His eyes crinkled into a teasing smile. "You've lost it, haven't you, and you're scared to admit it? But what do I care about the ring as long as I've got you? As soon as I'm mobile again, the first thing we'll do is to buy you another one."

"But . . ." she began in feeble protest.

Adam cut across her. "No 'buts,' darling. A new

ring will mark a new beginning for us." He studied her face appraisingly. "I do like your new hairstyle. It's sort of softer, more natural-looking."

Belinda felt a rising sense of panic. It was one thing to decide on this deception, but how could she possibly hope to keep it up when there were hazards at every turn waiting to trip her? A missing wedding ring, a different hairstyle. And total ignorance of this district and all the people living around here. She was likely to give herself hopelessly away with every word she uttered.

And yet . . . To go back now on her decision was unthinkable. She would have to muddle through somehow! So, forcing a smile, she ran her free hand through the loose auburn waves and told Adam she was glad he liked it this way.

"How's Belinda?" he asked suddenly.

Hearing her own name spoken gave her a jolt, but she recovered quickly and muttered that Belinda was fine, just fine.

"I hope you'll persuade her to come and visit us soon," Adam went on. "I'd like to see her again. We both owe that sister of yours so much, don't we, darling? But for her we'd never have met."

Quite unwittingly he was twisting a knife in Belinda's heart. "Sure," she said huskily. "We'll ask her to come for a weekend."

Adam pressed her hand. "I'm glad you've changed your mind about that. You seemed so much against the idea when you first heard she was coming to Britain, and I couldn't understand why."

A tap on the door saved Belinda from the need to comment. At Adam's "Come in" a dark-haired woman of about forty entered the room. She was a bit too thin, with a long narrow face and a rather beaky nose. Not knowing who she might be, Belinda smiled at her in a vaguely friendly way, but the woman acknowledged her with only a cool nod. She greeted Adam, though, with a bright smile that lent charm to her plain features.

"Hallo, Peg!" he said warmly. "Nice of you to drop by. What brings you into town?"

"Shopping I am!" she explained in a Welsh lilt. "I brought the Land Rover, with a list from everyone as long as your arm. Good it is to see you alive and kicking, Adam. You can't know how anxious we've all been. How do you feel?"

"A bit the worse for wear," he said ruefully, "but I'm making progress. I certainly feel a lot better now that Barbie's back," he added with a loving glance at Belinda. "You'll see, Peg, I'll be up and about again in no time at all."

"Now there's no cause to be hurrying yourself," she reproved him. "Huw Morgan has everything under control, indeed, with Gwillam and my da and young Davy to help him."

"So I'm not really needed at all up at Glyn-y-Fflur?" Adam quipped.

While they chatted Belinda had an opportunity to think, to try to come to terms with this new danger. She raked her memory for the meager titbits of information about the stud farm and its staff that Barbara had let drop in her occasional letters and during the past ten days in London. This would be Peg Phillips, whose husband and father and teenage son all worked at Glyn-y-Fflur. And Huw Morgan was Adam's stud groom. There was something else about Huw that she couldn't at once recall. Then it came to her. He wasn't married, but he lived in a bungalow with his elderly mother—no, his grandmother, who was totally blind.

Peg said good-bye to Adam and turned to the door. "Will I be telling Megan that you'll be wanting dinner tonight?" she asked Belinda stiffly.

Another frantic search through her memory ensued. Megan must be the woman who had kept house for Adam before his marriage and still came in each day to help Barbara. Her husband also worked for Adam on the stud farm. Belinda felt a shudder run down her spine. When deciding to stay on in the guise of Adam's wife she'd given no thought to where she'd spend tonight. Fortunately, she was rescued by Adam remarking at once, "I shouldn't go back to Glyn-y-Fflur, darling. You can stay over at the hotel here."

Relief flooded through her and must have shown on her face. While the woman looked even more disapproving, Adam said easily, "There'll be a bit more life for you here in town. You always complain that evenings at home are deadly dull."

Belinda blushed on her sister's behalf and tried to hide her embarrassment with a smile. It did nothing to redeem her in Peg's eyes, though, and she gave Belinda a sullen nod as she departed.

"There's a phone right here," said Adam, pointing at the bedside table. "Why not call the hotel now and book yourself a room?"

"Is that necessary?" Belinda stalled desperately. "I mean, they're not likely to be full at this time of year, are they?"

"Probably not, but it's best to make sure."

"Er . . . do you happen to know the number?"

"Sorry. But the directory is there, on the shelf below."

Oh, no! What was she going to do? Frantically she racked her brains. She recalled seeing a hotel from the taxi, but what on earth was its name? A bird, surely? Duck? No, swan. The Black Swan, that was it. She took the book from the shelf and flipped through the pages with a beating heart. Thank heaven she'd remembered it right! A number was listed for the Black Swan Hotel in Penystrad and she tried to get herself together as she dialed. It took a lot of nerve to book herself a room in the name of Mrs. Lloyd.

"There, that's fixed," said Adam as she hung up. "Now come and sit here beside me, darling, so I can put my arm round you. It's as if you're a million miles away, hovering out of reach like that."

"But, Adam," she protested uneasily, "you must take care."

He laughed. "Battered and bruised as I am, a little close contact with my wife is something that's definitely prescribed by Dr. Llewelyn. In fact, he wanted me to have you sent for yesterday."

Resignedly, but jumpy with nervousness, Belinda did as he said, perching herself on the very edge of the bed. Adam slid an arm about her slender figure and drew her softly to him with a sigh of pleasure. Belinda felt his breath warm on her cheek and she ached with longing to melt against him. It evoked tantalizing memories of those days in the Alpine ski resort, those few wonderful days before Barbara found herself suddenly without a man in tow and stole Adam away from her.

"I love you, darling," he murmured into the silky auburn tresses of her hair.

Belinda was silent, holding herself very still. After a moment he prompted, "Well, aren't you going to say it back?"

Before she was aware, the words had burst through her defenses. "I love you, Adam," she whispered softly, and it was nothing but the truth. But the look of happiness on his face was a terrible reproach to her conscience.

A young nurse entered carrying a folding bed tray set with tea things and arranged it across Adam's knees. An extra cup had been provided for Belinda.

"After you've had tea, Mrs. Lloyd," she said, "Dr. Llewelyn would like a word with you. His office is just along the corridor. You'll see his name on the door."

With every passing moment, Belinda thought desperately, she was digging a deeper pit for herself.

Dr. Llewelyn, a short man with iron-gray hair and gold-rimmed spectacles, looked up from the desk as Belinda entered his office. His expression was professionally neutral, but tending toward disfavor.

"Come in and sit down, Mrs. Lloyd. How's the hand?"

"The . . . the hand?"

"The one you injured when you took a tumble yourself," he said, impatiently reaching forward for her left hand. He gave it a perfunctory glance. "Not a mark! And you seemed to imagine that you'd be mutilated for life."

Belinda shrank inwardly, afraid to utter a word lest she give herself away. The doctor closed a file on his desk, leaned back and removed his spectacles, surveying her with a frown.

"That husband of yours took a considerably worse fall than you did, though mercifully there's no damage that's likely to be permanent. He was still unconscious when he was brought in here and he suffered quite a severe degree of shock. As I understand it, when he fell he got crushed between the horse's flank and the stone parapet of the bridge. It's a miracle that no bones were broken. All the same, there are quite a few badly torn muscles and ligaments."

"So I guess you'll want to keep him in hospital for a while longer?" Belinda queried.

Dr. Llewelyn rubbed his chin ruminatively. "There's no specific medical reason for keeping him here, and he's pressing me hard to discharge him. If I could rely on him to behave sensibly and take care

37

of himself I'd let him go home quite soon. But Adam Lloyd is a stubborn and strong-willed man, as you must know. Can I rely on you to see that he stays indoors and rests . . . really rests? Otherwise he could do himself a lot of harm."

Belinda moistened her lips and made an inarticulate response. It was as if the net of her own making was drawing closer about her, entangling her completely. In deciding to play out this charade she hadn't reckoned on having to take Adam home from the hospital. Nor had she really thought about the time factor. On Monday she would be expected to turn up for work. She would have to phone her boss and explain that there had been a family crisis.

"Well?" the doctor rapped.

"I . . . I'll do my best," she said faintly.

He rose to his feet and paced to the window, then swung round abruptly to face her again. "I'd better be blunt with you, Mrs. Lloyd. It will call for a great deal of sympathy and patience, a lot of tact and diplomacy, to control a man like your husband. He himself will be impatient with his disabilities and he's likely to become short-tempered and irritable. You must respond with firmness, but firmness without friction and argument, to ensure that he carries out the regime I have laid down for him. Are you capable of doing that?"

"Yes . . . yes, of course," Belinda stammered. "How can you doubt it, Dr. Llewelyn?"

He regarded her through narrowed eyes. "Your husband refused to have you sent for. It was as if he felt half-afraid you would object to returning from London earlier than planned and he didn't want that unpleasant fear confirmed."

"That's nonsense! Naturally I'll do everything in my power to help his recovery."

The doctor still hesitated, but finally he nodded. "Right, then, I'll discharge him the day after tomorrow . . . Monday. The sister will give you details of his treatment, and you'd better get the physiotherapist to show you how to massage his shoulders."

"Me . . . massage him?" Belinda gasped in dismay.

The doctor's doubts about her seemed to be reinforced. "Why not? There's nothing difficult about it. A twice-daily session will ease the pain considerably and help get your husband's musculature into trim again. Glyn-y-Fflur is too far away for the physiotherapist to travel back and forth, so it's up to you."

Judging by Dr. Llewelyn's attitude, Belinda realized the interview was at an end. Bewildered by the turn of events, she tried desperately to marshal her thoughts.

"How long will it be, Doctor, before Adam is back to normal?" she faltered.

He gestured impatiently. "That will depend largely on you, as I hope I've made clear. Now, if you'll excuse me, Mrs. Lloyd, I'm late for my rounds."

Out in the corridor again Belinda was seized with renewed panic. She was suddenly faced with a bewildering set of problems that she had never envisaged when she embarked so impetuously upon this deception. I'll just take one step at a time, she told herself sternly, matching her action to her thoughts as she made her way back to Adam's room on legs that felt limp and shaky. Right now I must plan what I have to do for the rest of the day. Then tomorrow. Monday, the day of Adam's return home, seemed too far away even to think about.

"Well, what's the verdict?" asked Adam as she went in and closed the door.

"Dr. Llewelyn said you had a very bad fall, Adam, and that it's very important for you to take things really easy for some time. He thinks you ought to stay here for a while longer. I think you should, too," she added forcefully. "It makes a lot of sense."

Adam shook his head. "Sorry, darling, that's just not on! The question is, when can I go home?"

Belinda sighed, seeing that Dr. Llewelyn had been right and it was a waste of breath trying to get Adam to change his mind. "He's agreed to discharge you on Monday," she told him.

"Monday! That's not bad. I know that Huw is perfectly competent to run the stud in my absence and he's utterly trustworthy. But all the same, I want to be back there where I can keep my finger on the pulse."

"The doctor was most insistent that you don't overdo things, Adam," she warned.

"And I won't," he promised airily. "I realize that I shan't actually be able to work with the horses for a while, but at least I can supervise. Any kind of business enterprise soon runs down if the boss man lets go the reins, and I've not built Glyn-y-Fflur to what it is today for the pleasure of seeing it lose its impetus." He saw the anxiety on Belinda's face, misinterpreted it, and his determined expression softened at once. Holding out a hand to her, he drew her close. "Don't worry, darling, I don't intend to make the same mistake again. I won't ever get so completely absorbed with the job that it gets in the way of our marriage."

"It . . . it's not that!" Belinda protested. But she could say no more, because Adam had pulled her closer and put his lips on hers in a tender, promising kiss that stabbed her through with longing. Her eyes filled with tears at the thought that this was stolen joy. A joy that must inevitably lead to even greater heartache in the end—for them both!

"Sweetheart," he murmured against her cheek, "I have this crazy notion that I'm falling in love with

you all over again. The way I feel right now, nobody
would ever guess that we're an old married couple
already coming up to our first wedding anniversary.
I want to make it a really marvelous celebration
when it comes, to show you how much I appreciate
you, Barbie. With luck, I'll be fit enough to ski again
by then and we'll be able to go on that vacation after
all, just as we planned. Only we'll make it more like
a second honeymoon, shall we?"

Belinda murmured something inaudible in reply.
She did not dare say more. The joy she had so briefly
felt at Adam's kiss was gone and her heart was
leaden now.

When Belinda left the hospital, carrying her small
weekend suitcase, she was able to walk unhesitating-
ly to the hotel. The Black Swan was an ancient
ivy-clad building with erratically set diamond-leaded
windows. Inside, there was oak paneling on the
walls, and huge oak beams, black with age, support-
ed the low ceilings. An appetizing aroma of food
drifted from the dining room.

She pinged the brass bell on the desk and after a
moment a small and rather stout woman emerged
from the nether regions. Seeing Belinda, she at once
adopted a cautiously welcoming smile.

"Good evening to you, Mrs. Lloyd. And how did
you find poor Mr. Lloyd, may I inquire?"

"He's still badly shaken up, of course, but he
seems to be on the mend. He's going to be discharged on Monday," she added.

"Now isn't that good news for you? So you'll be
wanting the room just two nights, then?"

"Er, yes . . . that's right."

The stout little woman led the way up the solid,
square-built staircase, puffing a bit from the exertion. "Dinner is being served up this minute, so
anytime you're ready to come down is fine, Mrs.

Lloyd." Throwing open a door on the upper landing, she added in a somewhat defensive tone, "I hope this will do."

The room was small but charming. Rose-patterned chintz covered what looked like a featherbed and the same fabric hung at the casement window.

"I think it's lovely," said Belinda. "Thank you."

She was awarded a look of pleased surprise and the woman withdrew. Belinda went to the window and stood looking out thoughtfully at the lamplit market square. There were few people about, now that the shops were closed, but even so she had received a number of greetings while she walked from the hospital . . . all wary smiles or cool nods. It was painfully clear that Barbara had not made herself popular with the townsfolk.

Entering the dining room was an ordeal. She smiled vaguely around the candlelit room, hoping this would suffice to acknowledge anyone whom she ought to appear to know. As she took her seat at the corner table indicated by the waitress a man sitting across the room stood up and came over. He was very good-looking, tallish, about forty, with a mass of fair hair worn rather long. He was dressed casually in a tweed jacket and white polo-neck sweater, and gave an impression of supreme self-confidence. He awarded Belinda a slow, ironic smile.

"And what, might I ask, has poor old Dorian done to merit the deep-freeze treatment?"

She looked at him nervously. "I'm sorry, I . . ."

"How's hubby?" he inquired. "I gather he came a really nasty cropper."

"Yes, but thank heaven he's doing very well," she faltered. "Dr. Llewelyn says that he'll be okay so long as he takes things easy and gets plenty of rest."

"Rest, eh? That will give you lots of lovely time on your hands!" He chuckled. "Couldn't be better! I arrived yesterday to spend a while at the cottage preparing scripts for my new series."

Fear clutched at Belinda's heart. This man, she sensed, represented danger in some unknown way. She hadn't a clue how she ought to deal with him.

"Don't look so scared, Barbie," he said easily. "I'm not going to embarrass you by joining you for dinner. But we are neighbors, so a friendly word in public is hardly a criminal offense. So smile and look pleased to see me, for heaven's sake."

"I . . . I'm sorry," she muttered again, summoning up the ghost of a smile.

She was saved by the waitress's voice calling from across the room. "Mr. Pettifer, your steak is ready. Would you like me to bring it over?"

"No, serve it there, Gwyneth," he called back. "I'm just coming." His blue eyes danced with devilry as they challenged Belinda in a long intent look. "See you soon, Barbie . . . very soon! And in more propitious circumstances. 'Bye for now!"

Covertly watching him through her lashes as he lounged away, Belinda realized why he'd looked vaguely familiar to her. Dorian Pettifer! She'd seen that Nordicly handsome face in a British travel series and she'd decided at the time that he was just a bit too good-looking to be trusted. So what exactly had been his relationship with her twin sister? She shuttered her thoughts, not wanting to reach any definite, unsavory conclusions.

At any other time she would have enjoyed her meal of roast duckling followed by apple pie and cream. But in her present state of nervous anxiety she quickly ate what little she could manage and rose to leave the dining room. On her way out she had to pass near Dorian Pettifer's table and she gave him a brief, cool nod. He was drinking wine with his cheese and raised his glass to her in a mocking salute.

Despite the deep quiet of the small Welsh town and the surrounding countryside, Belinda had little peace that night. She tossed and turned restlessly in the billowy featherbed and dawn found her at the window watching the sky lighten over the eastern mountains. What did the coming day hold for her? she wondered with dread.

By supreme concentration, by trying to anticipate the numerous problems before they actually confronted her, by adopting a vague smile when she didn't know the right answer to a question, Belinda managed to survive somehow. If she seemed rather absentminded, she just had to hope that it was put down to her concern over Adam.

During the morning he insisted on trying a short walk along the hospital corridor, with the aid of a walking tripod and leaning heavily on Belinda's arm. She realized how weak Adam still was when they returned to his room and he sank down thankfully onto the bed.

"It hurts like the devil!" he grumbled.

"You can't expect too much all at once," she reproved him quietly. "You've got to take things gently."

"Fat chance of doing anything else"—he grimaced —"with you reading the riot act to me every time I lift a finger."

"I'm only trying to tell you what's best for you," she protested.

"Listen," he said, "you can nag me as much as you like, Barbie darling. Just seeing you around is the finest tonic I could have. You know, I've got a feeling that going off to stay with Belinda was a darned good idea on your part. After this separation I see anew all the things about you that I first fell in love with."

"Do . . . do I seem much different from before I went away?" Belinda asked uneasily.

"Maybe we've both changed a bit," he suggested. "It could be that it needed something like this accident of mine to give us both a jolt . . . make us realize where we were heading. If that's the case, then it's the best thing that ever happened to me, short of meeting you in the first place!"

Lying back again on the pillows, Adam reached out for her. Belinda resisted momentarily, but the reproachful expression in his eyes overcame her qualms. If, over the next few days or however long it took, she was going to act out this charade, she could hardly hold back from kissing Adam when she was supposed to be his wife. So she allowed her stiff body to soften, and with a sigh of pleasure he drew her down to him and gave her a long, passionate kiss that left her dizzy with delight. Even when he finally let her go he kept his arm about her shoulders, his fingertips delving into the soft thickness of her hair to caress the skin at her nape.

"You have such beautiful eyes, darling," he murmured. "They remind me of Blaendyffryn when the sun first strikes it in the morning."

"Blaendyffryn?" she queried, momentarily off guard.

Adam drew back a little and regarded her with surprise. "You're always riding off on your own up that way. I thought it was your favorite part of Glyn-y-Fflur."

"Oh, yes. I wasn't thinking," she mumbled, shocked at being so nearly caught in yet another snare.

She was saved from any danger of Adam pursuing the subject by a tap on the door. In walked a cheerful, plumpish, dark-haired girl of about Belinda's own age, wearing a white overall-coat. Seeing the two of them so close together, she said with an amused grin, "That's a better sort of therapy, Mrs. Lloyd, than any I can offer to your husband. Still, I do have a few professional bits of know-how that I can show you."

Flushing, Belinda jumped up from the bed and stood smiling awkwardly.

"This is Elspeth Davies, darling," Adam explained. "She's the physiotherapist. I don't know if you two have ever met."

Instinctively Belinda began to shake her head. But she checked herself quickly when Elspeth said, "We did once, as a matter of fact. I was around when you were brought in last autumn with that injured finger."

"Yes, of course," Belinda said at once with an apologetic smile.

"But I'm not surprised that you don't really remember, Mrs. Lloyd. You were in rather a state that day, and in no mood for social chat." Turning briskly to Adam, Elspeth went on, "Now, we'll have your pajama jacket off so I can take a look at your back. That's it, roll over on your stomach."

When she had arranged him in a suitable position Elspeth took a tin of talc from her pocket and shook some out on her hand, smoothing it over the rippling muscles of Adam's broad shoulders and upper back. For Belinda, seeing him lying there half-naked, even with the physiotherapist in the room, was a step toward intimacy that she wasn't prepared for. Her heart began thudding wildly and she couldn't wrench her eyes away. As Belinda watched Elspeth begin the preliminary stroking movements across the smooth skin, her fingertips itched to touch him too. Yet at the same time she was filled with dread at the prospect of having to do precisely that in just a few minutes.

As Elspeth worked she explained exactly what she was doing and why. Long strokes at first to stimulate the circulation, then a series of pressing and kneading movements. "He's still pretty sore and tender, so you must go easy," she cautioned. "Now, you have a try."

Belinda hung back, scared to lay her hands on him. Elspeth said encouragingly, "Go on, don't be afraid. Just follow my instructions and you can't do any harm."

As Belinda's fingers made contact an extraordinary thing happened. It felt almost as if a mysterious sort of electric current was flowing through her. Adam, whose whipcord shoulder muscles were tense and unyielding at first, seemed to relax swiftly under her ministrations.

"You're doing fine," said Elspeth, surprise in her voice. "A real natural! Are you sure you've never had any kind of training in massage?"

Belinda shook her head. "No, none."

"Then you're a marvelously quick learner. What do you say, Mr. Lloyd? Can I safely leave you in your wife's hands?"

Adam twisted his head on the pillow and grinned up at them both. "I think you can rest content about that, Elspeth!" His dark gaze lingered on Belinda for a moment and she felt a sudden bubble of excitement. Recklessly mad as she knew this deception to be, it was becoming increasingly difficult to view it in that light. It seemed so right, so sensible, so obvious, that her place was here with Adam at this traumatic time, coaxing his fine body back to its normal state of physical perfection and shielding him from the shocking knowledge of his wife's treachery.

Working gently and rhythmically on Adam's shoulders, Belinda felt in a curious state of suspension from the bleak reality. Here and now was all that counted and her immediate path seemed clear. But it was a path that led into a foggy, shadowed future, with no visible end. She envisioned the next few days at Glyn-y-Fflur, where she would attend to his every need: massaging him like this, preparing tempting meals, smoothing out problems that arose, being his constant companion. But she knew only too well that in the shadows lay innumerable pitfalls and dangers just waiting for her.

"Well, I'll leave you to get on with the good work, Mrs. Lloyd," said Elspeth cheerfully. "I've got another patient to see before I can go home to my Sunday lunch."

Startled from her reverie, Belinda realized that she had scarcely been aware of Elspeth's presence during the past few minutes.

"Am . . . am I doing it properly?" she stammered.

"Like an expert! Give your husband a session each morning and evening and it'll do wonders for him. I'll drive over to Glyn-y-Fflur in a few days to see how he's progressing. 'Bye for now!"

When the door closed behind her and they were alone Belinda felt acutely self-conscious all of a sudden. She lifted her hands from Adam's back and stepped away from the bed.

"Hey!" he protested. "I'm entitled to another ten minutes yet. I'm not letting you get away with giving me short measure, darling."

"I . . . I'm sorry." She gulped.

Adam sighed with contentment as she resumed the massage. "It would hardly be tactful to make comparisons in front of Elspeth," he said laughingly, "but you do a lot more good for me than she does—in more ways than one! I reckon you must have the gift of healing hands. Funny that I've never had the least idea before. Earlier this morning it was torture to move, but now my shoulders feel a whole lot easier."

"I'm glad, Adam," she said huskily.

"Not half as glad as I am."

Ten minutes later, when she called a halt, Adam rolled over to face her. His dark eyes glittered with tenderness and love. "I'm only just beginning to realize how lucky I am and how much I was dreading that my luck had run out. I think I'd already subconsciously convinced myself that things were finished between us. Maybe that explains why I couldn't handle Apollo the other morning, because I wasn't concentrating properly. Part of me was so anxious about you."

Belinda was silent, her heart too full to speak.

"As it turned out, I wouldn't change a thing," he went on. "Even though that fall nearly killed me! You and I are together, Barbie . . . more so than ever before. It might all have been planned by a kindly providence—Belinda coming to Britain and you going to visit her. It's as if we needed that break from each other and the shock of me being injured. I know now, darling, that things aren't going to go wrong for us again. We've really found each other at last."

Standing beside the bed, Belinda turned her face away to hide the tears that pricked her eyes. Adam reached for her hand and drew her toward him with surprising strength. As his lips met hers in a lingering kiss it felt as if she were drowning in warm, dark waters. She closed her eyes and accepted her death sentence in a daze of bliss.

Chapter Three

The ambulance carrying Adam and Belinda left the little country town behind, following the winding main highway for a couple of miles, then turned onto a narrow byroad that climbed steeply. The winter morning was bright and crisp, the sun melting away the powdering of overnight frost that mantled the hedgerows.

At Adam's request Belinda had telephoned the house earlier on to announce that he was being discharged. Luckily she'd thought to look up the number while at the hotel, so she was prepared. Even so, she felt tense with nerves when she heard a lilting voice answer, "Good morning. Glyn-y-Fflur here."

"Is that, er . . . Megan?"

"Who else would it be, Mrs. Lloyd?" The tone had changed at once to one of cool hostility.

50

"Oh, yes, of course. Sorry." She felt flustered, aware that Adam was watching. "Er . . . I'm just calling to say that Adam is being discharged today. We'll be arriving at about one o'clock, I guess."

"Now that is good news, indeed!" But the woman added quickly, as if to remove any impression that she would be glad to see Adam's wife, "I mean that they're letting Adam out of hospital so soon."

"Yes, isn't it?"

"I'll have to be making some lunch for you. Is there anything special you want, Mrs. Lloyd?"

"No, I'll leave it to you. Something light and easy to digest would be best, please."

"I'll make it fish, then—there's plenty in the deep-freeze. And how about me doing a chicken for dinner this evening?"

It sounded as if Megan normally prepared all the meals at Glyn-y-Fflur, Belinda thought, though she'd better not take that for granted. "That sounds ideal," she said. "Thanks, Megan."

"Will that be all, Mrs. Lloyd?" Though the words were still clipped the tone of voice seemed somewhat mollified. Even slightly surprised, Belinda thought.

"Yes, I guess so."

As Belinda replaced the phone Adam said, "It would be nice if you could get on a bit better with Megan and the others. If you'd make that little extra effort, darling, like you did just then, you'd find they'd be more than willing to meet you halfway."

Without realizing it Adam had given her a warning that she couldn't expect to find herself popular at Glyn-y-Fflur. It was only too dismally apparent from the contacts she had so far made among people who had known her twin sister—Dr. Llewelyn, Peg and Megan—that Barbara hadn't been at all well-liked. She'd have to guard against being overly friendly, but she could hardly change her whole nature to fit in with the unflattering image they held of Adam's wife.

Earlier on she'd made another call, this time using not the phone in Adam's room, but the call box in the hospital lobby downstairs. Glancing around carefully to ensure that she couldn't be overheard, she'd dialed the number of Orbital Travel in London. Once put through to her boss, she explained that she'd been called away from London over the weekend. "I hate having to ask for time off when I've only just arrived in Britain, Mr. Bellamy, but this is a family emergency. Maybe I could have the vacation I was planning to take in August brought forward?"

"Well, of course, Belinda, if it's an emergency. I hope it's nothing too serious?"

"My brother-in-law has had an accident—a bad fall from his horse—and my sister is away traveling in the Far East. So . . ."

"Yes, I can see that's very difficult. You'd better just give me the number where we can reach you, Belinda, in case anything should arise."

Oh, no! It would never do if anyone called Glyn-y-Fflur asking for Miss Vaughn. "There's a bit of a problem, Mr. Bellamy," she said. "I mean, everything is rather unsettled at the moment and I'm not certain just where I'll be staying. But I'll be sure to keep in touch."

"If that's how it's got to be." Her boss didn't sound any too pleased. "Don't forget now, Belinda, and I hope that things go well with your brother-in-law."

"Thanks, Mr. Bellamy," she said, and hung up. That was one difficult hurdle crossed! Yet somehow the problem of her job in London seemed almost trivial compared with the ones she had to face right here in Wales.

* * *

As the ambulance drove on, climbing higher into the hills with every mile, the signs of habitation were fewer and fewer. At each roadside cottage they came to a face would appear at the window, suggesting that a passing vehicle was an event not to be missed. The landscape here, even in winter, was incredibly soft and green. Overhead, the bare branches of the trees on either side of the road entwined like latticework and Belinda guessed that in summertime this would be a lush green tunnel of foliage. Once she saw a mass of snowdrops in a little dell, their tender white bells nodding in the wind, and farther down the hillside a river sparkled in the crystalclear sunlight like a million diamonds. Ahead the mountains rose against a backdrop of pale-blue sky.

"It's so beautiful!" she breathed, a lump in her throat.

Adam, on his stretcher-bed, looked up at her in a puzzled sort of way. "That's a strange thing for you to say, darling."

Belinda bit her lip and murmured, "I guess it just kind of hit me, coming back after a break."

He pressed the hand that he was clasping in his. "Perhaps you're seeing it through completely new eyes. You always used to complain that this part of the world was like a desert, with hardly a single building to be seen."

Belinda smiled back at him awkwardly, knowing that her best hope of safety lay in silence. But it was difficult to remain silent a few miles farther on when they reached a point where the narrow road twisted between sheer bare rocks rising to jagged peaks around them, then dipped suddenly downward. Adam called to the driver, "Would you mind stopping here for a moment?"

He obligingly pulled up and cut the engine. Adam raised himself painfully on his elbows to look out of the ambulance window. Belinda helped support him and he smiled at her gratefully.

"Most times when I come through this pass I stop for a few minutes, just to drink in the view of Glyn-y-Fflur. Even after living here for seven years the beauty of this valley still gets to me. I know you can't see it in quite the same way, darling, but . . ."

Belinda wished she could tell Adam that his little Welsh valley was the most exquisite place she could imagine. But she was supposed to be her twin sister, and Barbara had taken quite a different view of Glyn-y-Fflur. To her it had been too remote and boringly dull. So, refraining from making a reply, Belinda gazed down in silent wonderment at the valley spread before them. It was girdled about by the mountains, whose wooded slopes ran down to the green meadows and paddocks of the stud farm. A river ran through it like a length of silver ribbon, hazed with winter mist. She could see, reduced to mere toy size at this distance, clusters of neat farm buildings, several bungalows and a fine old stone-built house whose windows reflected the slanting rays of the sun.

And in the paddocks were horses, lots of horses. Belinda's spirits soared in excitement. It was so long now since she'd had any contact with horses, though at one time they'd been the love of her life and she'd thought about them almost nonstop.

"Okay," said Adam, with a nod at the driver to move on again. "Thanks."

As the ambulance twisted its way downward the view of the stud farm constantly vanished behind rocks and trees, then reappeared, growing nearer all the time. Soon they were on the valley bottom, driving along a sandy track between neat white palings. A few moments later they drew up before the big house. On the steps outside the arched entrance porch a small group of people was gathered and Belinda's heart sank. These were people she was supposed to know very well, yet Peg Phillips was the only one she would actually recognize.

Was this to be the moment of her exposure? It would be a terrible time for Adam, overjoyed as he was about coming home, to learn that he'd been deceived. Somehow she had to bluff her way through the next few minutes.

Fortunately for Belinda, Adam himself came in for most of the staff's attention as the driver opened the ambulance's rear door and began to help Adam out.

"Hi, boss!" came from an elderly man who stood with Peg Phillips and a shyly smiling lad of sixteen or so. Peg's father and her son, Davy, Belinda guessed. Another man, with an air of greater authority about him, greeted Adam cheerfully after giving Belinda a quick, cautious glance of acknowledgment.

"It's good to see you back, Adam, and a lot sooner than any of us dared hope. But you must go easy and take good care of yourself for the present. There's nothing whatever for you to worry about except getting better. Everything here is under control."

Adam grinned back at him affectionately. "I'm sure it is, Huw. But I mustn't let you discover how unimportant I am in the running of this place!"

Huw Morgan, the stud groom, in other words, Adam's senior man. Of medium height and dark-haired, he looked lithe and fit, with a pleasant, squarish face and friendly brown eyes. Not at all the sullen, surly character that Barbara had described.

The remaining three people, she figured, must be Peg's husband, Gwillam, and Megan Williams and her husband, Dai. It was Megan whom Belinda regarded as the greatest danger to her here, since it was she who would have known Barbara the best. She was a short, plumpish woman of around forty-five, with round red cheeks and graying hair that was overpermed and frizzy. Greeting Adam warmly, she hardly spared more than a glance for Belinda.

As the ambulance drove off Belinda took Adam's arm and helped him mount the three steps to the front door with the aid of his crutches. Bracing herself, she called back over her shoulder, "Davy, will you bring the cases, please?"

"Yes, Mrs. Lloyd."

So the impersonation had passed unnoticed—for the moment! She had come through the first tricky confrontation. But pitfalls lurked at every turn, just waiting for a single incautious slip on her part. And here was one of the pitfalls right now. She had to act as if she knew her way around this house, yet she hadn't a clue which rooms the various doors belonged to.

It was Megan who unwittingly saved her, hurrying ahead of them and opening a door to the right. "You'll be wanting to get to bed right away, Adam," she said, "and I thought those stairs would be a problem for you just at present. So I got Dai to help me fix up a bed for you in the small living room. I hope it will do."

Thankfully Belinda helped Adam into the living room, which had been arranged very comfortably with a divan bed and bedside table. There was a TV set and also a sofa, but Belinda thought it probable that some of the usual furniture had been removed, because the room didn't look overcluttered. A cheerful log fire blazed on the open hearth.

"This is great, isn't it, darling?" said Adam, sinking down onto the sofa with a sigh of relief.

"Fantastic!" she agreed. "Thanks so much, Megan."

The woman looked astonished. "Well, glad I am that I did the right thing!" She might well have added, It makes a change for *you* to show approval, but instead she merely asked, "Is there anything either of you wants before I get the lunch?"

"I could use a drink," Adam said. "A nice cool beer, perhaps."

Belinda was firm and emphatic. "The doctor advised no alcohol for a few days, so that's out!"

"Well, it was worth a try," said Adam, grinning ruefully. "How about you, darling? A Bloody Mary?"

She shook her head. "No, I don't want anything."

"There's no need to deprive yourself just because I can't join you."

"But I hardly ever . . ." she began, then hastily amended that to "I don't really feel in the mood for a drink at the moment. I can always change my mind later, can't I?"

"Sure."

"Now I must get you into bed," she said, becoming brisk. "That journey must have tired you."

"Let me help," offered Megan.

"Thanks, but there's no need. I can manage okay." As the woman looked resentful Belinda added smilingly, "I've had a lot of practice these past two days and I've gotten the hang of it."

"I'm glad you sent her away, darling," said Adam when the door closed behind the retreating Megan. "She's very willing, but just a bit ham-fisted. Whereas you . . . you've got the touch of an angel. Come on, give me a welcome-home kiss before you hoist me into bed."

Belinda steeled herself against showing any reluctance, against betraying that to her this was more than just a casual, everyday sort of affectionate kiss between a husband and wife. Yet even so, as she bent over and put her lips to his, it was all she could do not to slide her arms around his neck and crush herself against him.

"You're so good for me!" he sighed pleasurably and laughed. "I'm warning you, Barbie, that I'll be requiring frequent doses of this sort of treatment!" His fingers tightened their grip on her shoulders. "I can hardly wait till I—"

Belinda drew back hastily. "Come on, let's get that dressing gown off and have you tucked up in bed before Megan returns with the lunch."

She tried hard to be calmly practical, but the very act of laying hands on his hard-muscled body brought with it shivers of sensual excitement. By the time Adam was lying down beneath the covers he looked pale and drawn. When he turned to gaze out the window at the limpid blue sky Belinda covertly studied his profile: the dark hair, tousled now; the straight nose and determined jawline; the deep-set eyes and generous, sensitive mouth. He was suffering more pain than he admitted to, she realized, and it seemed very poignant to her that such a huskily built man, normally so strong and virile, should be reduced to the status of an invalid.

From a little way off came the sharp whinny of a horse, and Adam said with a faint smile, "That'll be Sharima in a tantrum about something that doesn't please her. Like every female that ever was!"

"You seem to have a low opinion of us," Belinda observed.

Adam turned back to her quickly and his dark eyes burned into her. "On the contrary! Oh, Barbie, it feels so good, you and I being in tune with each other like this. Promise me, if I do get a bit sharp or irritable while I'm laid up, that you won't hold it against me."

"Of course I won't," she assured him. "It must be so frustrating for you to be struck down like this."

His lips quirked in a meaningful smile. "You don't know just *how* frustrating, with you looking so desirable and me not being able to do much more than look at you."

A tap on the door announced Megan's arrival with their lunch, grilled sole and creamed potatoes garnished with tomatoes and green peas. There was a vanilla-flavored egg custard to follow. When they'd finished, Belinda carried the tray out to the kitchen, guided by the enticing aroma of perking coffee. It was a large, light room, well fitted with every modern appliance.

"That was delicious," she said, setting the tray down on a counter beside the dishwasher. It was obvious from Megan's raised eyebrows that she suspected sarcasm. "A good *plain* cook is what I am, Mrs. Lloyd, and I'll never be able to manage those fancy foreign dishes you're always wanting."

Oh, dear! Keeping her left hand carefully out of sight so that Megan wouldn't notice the absence of a wedding ring, Belinda smiled brightly. "Is that our coffee? Why don't I take it?"

"As you wish, Mrs. Lloyd. I'll be off home, then, if there's nothing more. And I'll be back later to see to your dinner as usual."

"Yes, fine."

Later, when Huw Morgan came over to see Adam and talk business, Belinda left them alone together, seizing her opportunity to look around the house and get her bearings. Downstairs, apart from the small living room she had just left, there was a spacious lounge furnished with comfortable armchairs and sofas and low occasional tables, the windows offering a fine view across the paddocks down the entire length of the valley. Next to this was the dining room, done in a modern style with teak furniture. On the walls hung numerous paintings of horses that presumably had been raised at the stud.

Across the hall she found what was clearly Adam's study-cum-office. A large desk was untidily scattered with papers and bookshelves lined two walls. A somewhat battered leather armchair looked as if it was much used. In addition there were also large walk-in storage cupboards, a laundry room and a cloakroom.

Ascending the curving staircase, Belinda came to a wide landing lit by two long windows. After just a quick glance around each of the four guest rooms she lingered in the master bedroom at the front of the house. This was much larger than any of the others, with a bathroom en suite. Strangely, it was the only room in the house to bear any recognizable signs of Barbara's taste, as if only here had she troubled to imprint her presence. The color scheme was dusky-pink and gold, the king-size bed swathed in a filmy canopy of voile. Underfoot was a silky shag carpet in a warm tone of ivory, and the window drapes were of brocaded satin. The total effect was one of flamboyant, sensuous luxury. It had always been the same, Belinda reflected, with her twin sister's way of dressing. Though Barbara had the flair for wearing clothes that one would expect in a fashion model she tended to spoil the overall effect by rather too much showiness.

Thinking of clothes, Belinda crossed to the closets that lined one entire wall, the mirrored doors reflecting the pale winter sunshine. The first one she opened contained racks of Adam's things—several suits, casual slacks of all kinds and various sweaters and sports jackets. She reached down one of the latter, a lightweight tweed in gray herringbone. Dreamily she fingered the fine fabric for a moment, then put its rough texture against her cheek. With a little shiver she put it back and firmly closed the sliding door.

The rest of the closets were reserved for Barbara. Row upon row of every kind of outfit hung there, many of them seeming hardly to have been worn. Belinda ran her hand along, separating the garments and glancing at each of them. A pink mohair rollneck dress appealed to her and she drew it out, holding it against herself and studying the effect in the mirror. Naturally it would fit her . . . their clothes had always been completely interchangeable, a source of much irritation to Belinda in their teenage days when Barbie was constantly grabbing her new purchases without asking permission.

Belinda hesitated, considering the pleated brown skirt and canary-yellow sweater she was wearing. This, plus a soft green woolen dress for the evenings and a pair of jeans and a thick pullover in case she had a chance to ride, was all she'd brought with her for just the weekend's stay she had anticipated. It looked as if the tables were turned now and she would be the one borrowing without permission. Oh, well, Belinda thought wryly. She was supposed to be Barbara and it would lend conviction to her pretense if she was wearing her sister's clothes.

Ten minutes later Belinda's new image was complete, her hair brushed in a halfway compromise between her own casual style and Barbara's more sophisticated swept-up arrangement, and her makeup applied from the wide range on the dressing table. No lipstick, though. None of her sister's colors was right for her, Belinda decided; all of them were just a shade too loud.

Yet even when wearing Barbara's dress she didn't feel a bit like her sister. Perhaps this was because it was one of the less flamboyant garments in Barbara's wardrobe. In fact, this was much the sort of thing she might have chosen for herself . . . given the cash to buy anything so obviously expensive.

After making her way downstairs she encountered Huw in the hall.

"Going already?" she asked with a smile.

"Ah, well, there's plenty for me to be getting on with," he replied, giving her a rather strange look.

"I was just going to make Adam some tea. Won't you stay and have a cup?"

"You're offering me tea?" he said incredulously.

"Yes, why not?"

Huw hesitated, but seemed to decide against saying whatever he had in mind. Instead he remarked, "Don't you think you ought to engage a nurse for a week or two to help you to look after Adam?"

"Thanks, but I can manage perfectly well," she replied, stung by his implied criticism.

"Can you, though, Barbara? It's not just a matter of making him a pot of tea now and then and soothing his fevered brow. You'll be at his beck and call all the time . . . and much though I admire Adam, I can't pretend that he's the most patient of men."

"I can manage," Belinda repeated stubbornly. Then, to show Huw that he couldn't expect to push her around, she added in a cool tone, "Didn't you say you had a lot to do?"

His eyes turned stony. "I did! And I'll see that it's done—without any reminders from you."

As he strode out, leaving her standing there, Belinda felt thoroughly wretched. Yet what did it really matter if she couldn't get along with Adam's senior man—or the rest of the staff, for that matter? She was here for one purpose and one purpose only: to see Adam through the worst of his injuries until he was strong enough to bear the harsh fact that the wife he adored had callously deserted him.

Belinda made a pot of tea, welcoming this chance to find her way around the kitchen. She discovered a

62

few small currant cakes to go with it and carried the tray through to Adam's room.

He was reading some correspondence that Huw must have left with him, but he thrust the letters aside and smiled at her.

"Tea! That's thoughtful of you, darling. I was just thinking how much I'd like a cup and wondering whether to ask you to make some."

Belinda put the tray down and said earnestly, "Anything you want, Adam, just tell me. I like doing things for you."

He studied her face almost disbelievingly, she thought. Then he asked, "What made you put on that particular dress, Barbie?"

"Don't you like it?" she asked, covering her nervousness with a smile.

"It's not *me* who doesn't like it, darling, it's *you!* I don't think I've seen you wear it once since the day I bought it for you last autumn."

Pouring the tea with a shaking hand, Belinda desperately sought a way out of yet another tricky situation. She said with an easy laugh, "Sorry about that, Adam! But it's not really so odd; I've got whole closets full of clothes. If I wore something different every single day it would take me weeks to work my way through them all."

Adam seemed highly amused. "Yet every time we're going out anywhere you complain that you've nothing fit to wear." His glance became more intent and penetrating. "Never mind, I'm glad you saved that dress for today, darling. You look really terrific, very, very sexy!"

Belinda colored violently and was unable to stop the cup of tea from rattling in its saucer as she handed it to him.

Later Adam reminded her that he was due for another massage. Belinda had been dreading this. It had been embarrassing enough at the hospital, but she guessed that in the privacy of home Adam would be less inhibited in his reactions. She managed to delay until she heard Megan arrive to start preparing dinner. At least that would give her a chaperon of sorts!

Adopting a brisk, professional approach, she helped Adam off with his pajama jacket and made him roll facedown on the bed. Then she shook talcum onto her hand, spread it over his naked shoulders and began the slow, rhythmical strokes just as Elspeth had demonstrated. She tried to keep her emotions in check, tried to keep her mind from dwelling on the intimate aspects of what she was doing, but she couldn't prevent herself from feeling little shivers of sensual excitement as she stroked his bare flesh. And all the while Adam delighted in it, sighing with pleasure.

"It's sheer bliss, darling," he murmured. "Not to mention the fact that all my aches and pains seem to melt away like magic when you do that."

After they'd eaten their dinner of chicken in cream sauce, and a raspberry mousse, Belinda and Adam watched television. Sitting beside his bed in the softly lit room, her hand tightly clasped in his, Belinda wandered off into a dreamy reverie. Outside a keen wind could be heard gusting around the corners of the house, but inside it was beautifully cozy and warm . . . just the two of them alone together now that Megan had returned to her own bungalow. Last winter, less than a year ago, this had been her idyllic vision of what her life with Adam would be, for she had been confident that he would ask her to marry him. Then Barbara had intervened and snatched her lovely dream away!

It was apparent that Adam loved Barbara devotedly, despite the fact that their marriage hadn't been all roses. But he didn't yet know of Barbara's ruthless rejection of him for another man. When he did learn of it, would he still love her? Probably, Belinda acknowledged with a bitter ache in her heart. Adam would be shattered, of course, but he'd most likely blame himself for failing to give his wife the kind of life that she thought she had a right to expect. Adam Lloyd was that sort of man.

Unknowingly, Belinda let out a long sigh, and Adam squeezed her hand. "What is it, darling? Why so sad?"

"Oh . . . nothing!"

"You're not bored?" he asked anxiously.

"Of course I'm not bored! I could go on sitting here like this for . . ." She stopped then added with a little laugh, "Unfortunately, though, it's high time I got you settled for the night. I'll leave the door open, so if you should wake up and need anything just ring that hand bell."

His dark eyes gleamed with naked desire. "I wish you didn't have to go upstairs, Barbie. Or rather, I wish to heaven that I could come up with you."

"Well, you can't," Belinda said sharply, adding, "And you never will be able to, unless you follow the doctor's instructions to the letter!" What on earth, she wondered desperately, had possessed her to say that?

Adam didn't miss his opportunity. With a laugh he said, "Was there ever a better incentive held out to a man to get fit quickly? The night I return to our bed upstairs, darling, will be a cosmic event. That's a promise!"

It was quite a while before he would let Belinda escape him. There was no sign of weakness in the way he held her captive in his arms, crushing her breasts against his chest, and the tingling imprint of his lips remained with her as she ascended the staircase. For a long time she stood at the window of her bedroom, staring out at the velvet blackness of the winter night. A few nearby lights stabbed across the darkness from the homes of the stud farm's staff. They seemed infinitely far away, though, beyond her reach. She felt dreadfully isolated, a cheating impostor there under false pretenses.

Chapter Four

In contrast to Belinda, Adam had slept excellently.

"It's being home with you, Barbie," he told her cheerfully as they were eating the breakfast Megan had prepared. "I feel that I'm definitely on the mend now. As it's such a lovely morning I'll get you to drive me around the place to take a look at things."

The very idea filled Belinda with panic. As yet she'd had no chance to familiarize herself with the layout of the farm. She said quickly, "It's far too soon to think of anything like that, Adam. The most you should attempt for the next day or so is just to get around the house a bit."

"Listen, Barbie, I know what I can manage and what I can't," he returned impatiently. "All I'm asking you to do is help me into the car and drive it. Is that too much?"

Tact and diplomacy would be called for, Dr. Llewelyn had rightly warned, to cope with such outbursts of frustrated irritability. Belinda suspected that sympathy would be of little use in the present instance. This was an occasion that called for a firm stand.

"You're going to do as I say and stay home," she told him flatly. "I'll be the one to decide when you're well enough to venture outside."

For several moments Adam glared at her mutinously. Then he shrugged a laugh. "Quite the little autocrat, aren't you? Oh, well, I suppose I'd better learn to be bossed around by my wife with good grace."

"I'm only acting in your best interests, Adam."

"I know you are, darling," he said with a loving look. "And it gives me a marvelous feeling to have you so concerned about me."

After breakfast she returned the tray to the kitchen, then nervously set about massaging Adam's shoulders again. Eventually this would become a matter of sheer routine and not be so unnerving, Belinda tried to tell herself consolingly. But judging from Adam's reactions as her hands slid over his rippling muscles, she feared that these twice-daily sessions would become considerably more of a problem rather than less.

When it was over, Belinda left Adam to catch some more sleep. This was an opportunity for her to look around the farm and cram her mind with the things she was supposed to know about it. After putting on a quilted parka and a pair of low-heeled shoes, she wandered outside into the sunshine. It was a morning of ineffable beauty, with warmth in the sun's rays even though the air was crisp and frosty. She breathed in deeply, the air as headily intoxicating as wine.

Beyond the lawns and flowerbeds surrounding the

house, sandy tracks led between white palings to various buildings: a huge Dutch barn, some smaller sheds and a great number of horse boxes. In each of the paddocks groups of mares and yearlings were grazing contentedly. Belinda stood at one of the gates, watching admiringly, and several of the ponies came toward her in friendly greeting. While she was stroking their velvet muzzles and whispering soft endearments she heard a scuffling noise behind her and a couple of quick yelps. She swung round to see a pair of lovely golden retrievers racing toward her.

A shout rent the air. "Bess, Tiger! Heel!"

Trained to instant obedience, the two dogs gave her a look of apology and returned to their master, following close on his heels as he came strolling over to her.

"Good morning, Huw!" she greeted him.

Huw Morgan nodded, unsmiling. "Sorry about that, Barbara. They should have known better."

"But Bess and Tiger weren't doing any harm," she said, grateful to him for supplying their names like that.

"I agree. But you hate dogs, so I always try to keep them from bothering you."

Oh, dear! Almost another slipup on her part. She should have remembered that Barbie had never shown any liking for dogs. As a child she had even been scared of them.

"Hate is rather too strong a word," Belinda said cautiously. "It's just that dogs and I don't get along too well."

"You could have fooled me," Huw remarked, indicating two furiously wagging tails. "It seems they've decided to forget the past and make fresh overtures of friendship." Mercifully Huw changed the subject as he and Belinda strolled together toward the stud-farm buildings, asking, "What sort of night did Adam have?"

"Oh, very good. He says he slept right through."

"I'm glad to hear it." Huw gave her a thoughtful glance. "Not you, though, apparently. From the look of you, I was expecting to hear that you'd spent most of the night sitting up with Adam."

"Oh, no! But I didn't sleep any too well," she admitted.

"I wonder why not?"

She sought for a plausible answer to give him. "Maybe because it's so quiet here after the noise of London."

"*Too* quiet, you mean?"

"I didn't say that!"

"You didn't need to say it. You've complained about it plenty of times before."

Belinda kept silent as they walked through an arched entrance to a paved yard that was lined with loose boxes. From a larger one set a little apart, a black stallion surveyed them interestedly from above the half-door. She was about to exclaim on what a magnificent head he presented, with his broad forehead and wide jaw, his bold but gentle eyes, then checked herself. This stallion, like all the other horses here, was an animal she was supposed to know well. So she contented herself with going forward to pat his muzzle, the stallion accepting her attentions with obvious pleasure.

"Well, I'll be jiggered!" said Huw.

"What's the matter?" Belinda asked, glancing round at him warily.

"I'd have thought that you wouldn't want to get within ten yards of Apollo," he explained.

Apollo! The stallion that had thrown Adam. And Barbara, too, earlier on. But this horse seemed to have no vice in him. For a prideful stallion he seemed remarkably good-natured. She felt no fear of him whatever and she refused to pretend to any. Continuing to pat him, she remarked, "Adam said there was a low-flying plane around when he was thrown. Apollo must have been startled by that."

Huw regarded her skeptically. "You know just where it happened, I suppose?"

"Er . . . by the footbridge, he told me."

"That's right. Yet you have the nerve to maintain it was all due to the noise of a low-flying plane? The plane, Barbara, was just the final straw for Apollo."

"I don't know what you mean," Belinda faltered.

"You know perfectly well what I mean! Adam was having difficulty taking Apollo over the bridge, and it's not surprising after your mishandling of him there."

"My . . . mishandling?"

"Don't play the innocent with me! I happen to have seen precisely what occurred that time Apollo threw you at the same spot. You were in a nasty mood that day, Barbara, and you were taking your bad temper out on the horse. Apollo needs a firm hand, I agree, but you can't expect any stallion to tolerate being kicked and lashed like that. It's lucky for you that he decided to bolt when he'd thrown you, rather than turn on you and trample you to death."

Belinda stared at him, appalled by what she was hearing.

"Horses have a long memory," Huw went on, "so it's not surprising that Apollo has always been difficult at that spot ever since. And the other day poor Adam had to suffer for what you did. In the normal way he can always handle Apollo, even when he's being temperamental. But like I said, that fool pilot flying too low was the final straw."

So Adam's accident was all due to Barbara! But Adam himself obviously didn't appreciate the sinister link between the two incidents. It was no wonder Barbara had been so reluctant to talk to him about her own accident with Apollo at the footbridge.

"How . . . how come you never told Adam what you saw?" Belinda stammered.

Huw regarded her with cold contempt. "Would you expect me to break it to Adam that his wife is the kind of woman who thinks nothing of mistreating his prize stallion? It's been a bit on my conscience that you might do the same sort of thing again, with some other mount, but I figured that you'd learned a lesson you wouldn't forget in a hurry."

From Huw's challenging expression it was obvious that he expected her to strike back. Doubtless Barbara would have done so, but Belinda was too shocked to manage any kind of answer.

After a few moments Huw went on in a less aggressive tone. "I must say, though, that Apollo seems to have forgiven you. Heaven knows why, but he's as docile with you as a lamb. And Bess and Tiger, too. Up to now they've always been very wary whenever you've appeared on the scene."

"I think you're exaggerating," she murmured awkwardly.

"Am I?" He shrugged. They had turned out of the yard and were approaching a neat, white-painted modern bungalow. A small bush of wintersweet stood beside the front door, defying the cold weather, its tiny yellow flowers scenting the air. Huw said, "Gran will have my elevenses ready by now. There's no point asking you to come in and have a cup of tea with us, is there?"

"Why not?" said Belinda, surprising herself and clearly surprising Huw, too, from the curious look he turned on her.

"Then do! It's not a lot of company the old lady gets."

Inside, the bungalow was spotless and smelled of beeswax polish. A large wood-burning stove in the living room-cum-kitchen warmed the whole house.

"Good morning, Mrs. Morgan," Belinda said

hesitantly to the white-haired old lady who was
filling a teapot from a large kettle. She was very tiny,
dressed all in black, with pursed lips and shriveled
cheeks.

"Who is this?" she demanded in a thin, piping
voice. Unlike a sighted person, she turned her ear
rather than her eyes to the doorway, and from her
puzzled expression Belinda wondered if she were a
little deaf as well as blind.

"It's Mrs. Lloyd, Gran, come to have a cup of tea
with us," said Huw.

"Mrs. Lloyd, is it?" The old woman frowned,
looking none too pleased. "And me not expecting a
visitor! Hurry you, Huw Morgan, and get the best
china from the cupboard."

"No need to worry, Gran," he said easily. "I'll
just be getting another cup and saucer down from
the dresser."

"No need to worry, indeed, and Mrs. Lloyd with
us! Quick now, Huw, and do as I say."

"Please, Mrs. Morgan," Belinda said hastily, "I
don't want you to go to any special trouble for me.
Besides, I think your everyday china is very attractive. I've always liked the willow pattern."

The old woman shrugged and returned to making
the tea. It was obvious that she felt very ill-at-ease.
"Sit you down, then, Mrs. Lloyd," she said after a
moment. "Bad news it is about your husband, but
Huw tells me that Mr. Lloyd is making good progress."

"Yes, he seems to be doing very well, considering." Belinda was wondering wretchedly if Huw had
told his grandmother the dreadful story of Barbara's
ill treatment of Apollo. It would account for the old
woman's guarded manner toward her.

The dogs had come in and flopped with sighs of
contentment in the best position on the hearth rug
by the stove. As Belinda stepped over them and took

a seat Mrs. Morgan said with a jerk of her head, "Try one of those griddle cakes on the plate there."

"Thank you." Though not hungry, Belinda took one out of politeness, balancing it in the saucer of the cup of tea Huw handed her. It was something between pastry and a cookie, with currants in it. She broke off a piece and popped it into her mouth. "This is very good," she commented sincerely. "Your own baking, Mrs. Morgan?"

"Indeed, yes."

"It must be difficult for you," Belinda said. "I . . . I mean . . ."

"Being without the sight of my eyes, you mean? That's so, but not as difficult as you might think. Making the griddle cakes is something I've done since the time I first helped my mam when I was a small girl and I just let my hands do it in the same way." Old Mrs. Morgan hesitated, then asked, "And how did you enjoy your visit to your sister in London?"

Belinda felt suddenly nervous, as if somehow threatened by the question. "It was wonderful to see her again after all this time," she said guardedly.

"A shock it must have been for her, too, when you told her about Mr. Lloyd's accident?"

"Told her . . . ?"

"You will have telephoned her, I'm thinking, about such unhappy news."

"Oh! Oh, yes, of course. From the Black Swan Hotel," she added quickly, making a mental note to pretend to call "Belinda" again this evening. It was an aspect she hadn't thought about, but Adam would consider it strange if his wife's twin sister didn't expect to be kept in the picture about his progress.

Huw, looking faintly puzzled, kept glancing from her to his grandmother and back again, but he made no attempt to join in the conversation. After a few more awkward exchanges with the old lady Belinda drained her cup and stood up.

"I must get back now," she said. "My husband might be wanting me for something. Thank you for the tea, Mrs. Morgan, and the delicious griddle cake."

Huw rose to his feet also, followed by the two scrambling dogs. "You must come in for tea another day, Barbara," he said with a friendly smile.

From her rocking chair by the stove Mrs. Morgan observed, "Doubtful it is that Mrs. Lloyd will be doing that, Huw. Go you now and show the lady out."

Filled with a vague apprehension she couldn't pinpoint, Belinda walked briskly back to the house. A yellow sports car stood outside and she wondered who it might belong to. As she drew near, the tall figure of Dorian Pettifer emerged from the front door. Spotting her, he waited by his car, lounging against it easily.

"We wondered where you'd got to," he called.

"We?" she queried, gripped by dismay.

"Your husband and myself. I thought it only neighborly to drop by and see how the invalid was progressing."

"I wish you hadn't," she said uneasily.

His blue eyes mocked her. "Not much of a welcome for a very good friend! I promise that you'll receive a much warmer welcome when you call on me, Barbie. When will that be, by the way? I'm growing quite impatient."

"Don't be absurd. I can't possibly visit you," Belinda told him in a stiff voice.

The blue eyes, still smiling, took on the color of ice chips. "You found no difficulty before, my love."

"Things are . . . different now. You must realize that."

"I'd have thought that having your husband safely

confined to the house would make it easier to get away, not harder. So I'll expect you this afternoon for a cozy cup of tea."

"Don't bother expecting me, Dorian. I won't be coming."

"Then I'll have to persuade you, shan't I?"

She shook her head vehemently. "I don't care how often you ask me, it won't make any difference."

"But I'm not asking you, sweetheart. I'm *persuading* you!"

Belinda tried to conceal her agitation. "If I say I'm not coming there's nothing you can do to make me."

"Think so?" Absently Dorian twirled his bunch of keys on his finger. "I guess that we've both been very careful here, Barbie, but you seem to forget that you wrote me a most passionate little letter when I was away filming in Africa, saying how terribly you missed having me around. I was very affected by the sentiments expressed . . . and I've no doubt your husband would be, too, in a rather different way!"

"That's blackmail!" Belinda gasped.

Dorian smiled in derision. "Like I said, I call it persuasion."

As he opened the car door to get in Belinda impulsively reached out and touched his arm. "Be reasonable, Dorian. You must see that with things as they are I can't possibly . . ."

"It's not as if Adam was on the danger list," he argued. "He told me that he's making fine progress . . . improving by the hour." Dorian paused and regarded her calculatingly. "Okay, I'll be 'reasonable,' as you put it. We'll give it a couple of days. After that I'll definitely expect some action. *Ciao!*"

Belinda stood watching him drive off, the wheels of his sports car spurting gravel. Turning to go into the house, she saw a movement at an upstairs window. Megan! She couldn't possibly have overheard their actual words at such a distance, but what might she have surmised from seeing them together? What, Belinda thought with sudden dread, might Megan already have known about Barbie's relationship with Dorian Pettifer? And how about the other members of the staff?

One tiny consolation, at least, was that Adam didn't appear to have any suspicions. This was confirmed a moment later when, with considerable trepidation, she entered his downstairs bedroom.

Adam flipped off the transistor radio he'd had on for the news and held out his hand to her, smiling. "Been for a stroll, darling? I'm glad. I'd hate to think I was keeping you housebound. Why don't you go for a ride this afternoon?"

"I . . . I'll see how I feel."

She went forward, nervously offering her lips for the kiss Adam obviously expected, and he held her pinned there. Against her will Belinda found herself responding and she felt a sense of helpless despair. Could she dare to hope, when she finally told Adam the truth, that he would accept the fact that she had only been acting in his best interest by playing out this macabre charade as her twin sister? Or would he turn on her in bitter resentment for deceiving him? She loved him so much that the thought of this was unbearable.

"You're so good for me, Barbie," he murmured as he let her go. "I must admit that I was wishing you were here a few moments ago. Dorian Pettifer called in. It was good of the chap to bother, I suppose, but I always find him such a bore. He's much too full of himself and his own cleverness."

Belinda gave a neutral sort of smile and said casually, "I saw Dorian just now as he was leaving and we stopped to exchange a few words."

"He told me he'd be staying at Tyfawr Cottage for a week or two this time. We'd better invite him over to dinner or something as soon as I'm up and about again. It's only neighborly."

Appalled, Belinda said quickly, "Surely there's no need to ask him over, Adam. I mean, he's supposed to be here for peace and quiet to do his writing, isn't he?"

Adam looked at her with surprise. "But you've always been so keen on having him to dinner before, darling, whenever he's been staying here."

Belinda felt a cold shiver run down her spine. Had it been some sort of black joke on Barbara's part, bringing her husband and her lover face to face over the dinner table? It was just the sort of mad risk her twin would delight in.

"Well, there's no need to invite him *this* time, Adam," she said, trying to sound firm and decisive. "Not until you're a hundred percent fit, anyway."

Against her advice, Adam insisted on sitting at the dining-room table for lunch. But afterward Belinda noticed how pale and drawn his face was.

"This afternoon you'd better rest lying down," she told him firmly.

"Okay, boss!" he agreed, smiling ruefully. When Adam was settled he said with a glance out of the window, "That sunshine looks very inviting. So off with you and have a nice ride, darling."

"But I can't leave you on your own, Adam, in case you need something."

"It's okay. You're forgetting that Tuesday is one of the days that Megan works right through, so she'll be on call."

"Oh, yes, of course!"

Adam smiled at her. "Huw will be glad for you to exercise one of the ponies. But not Apollo!" he added warningly.

"No," she said with an involuntary little shudder. "Not Apollo!" But the danger for her in riding Apollo would not be that he might misbehave, but that he *wouldn't.* And that would betray her completely.

Before going upstairs to change Belinda paused to study a framed, large-scale map of the area which hung in the hall. It was better to pinpoint the enemy, she thought, to know exactly where Dorian Pettifer's cottage was so that she could carefully avoid going anywhere near it. After quite a search she found the name Tyfawr. It seemed to be situated high in the lonely hills just beyond the far end of Glyn-y-Fflur, standing quite alone. To get there by road through the pass would be a distance of several miles, but Belinda guessed that it was possible to ride to it more directly. Had that been Barbara's method of visiting her lover?

There was a beautifully tailored riding outfit in her sister's wardrobe and Belinda hesitated over whether she ought to put it on. But she decided that for an everyday ride jeans and a parka would probably be Barbara's choice. Carrying a hard hat, she made her way down to the kitchen, where Megan was sitting at the table cleaning silver.

"I'll be out riding for an hour or so," Belinda told her. "You'll keep an ear open in case Adam wants anything, won't you?"

In reply she received a curt nod from Megan. Oh, well, she thought with a sigh, to be unpopular was what she had to expect and it was foolish to let it get her down. There were quite enough other things to worry about.

She found Huw in the yard, talking to Peg Phillips' son, Davy. He broke off at once and waved the lad away.

"So you're going riding," he observed dryly, his brown eyes watchfully on her face. "Which mount d'you want saddled?"

"I . . . I'll leave that to you," she said awkwardly. "I mean, whichever pony you want exercised."

"You've always favored Jasmin," he said thoughtfully.

"Okay, Jasmin will do fine."

He called Davy back and gave the lad instructions. "And I'll take Lady Luck myself."

Her heart sank at the realization that Huw Morgan intended to accompany her. This morning she felt she had coped quite well with him, but there was a strangeness about his manner toward her this afternoon that made her feel distinctly uneasy.

Five minutes later they set out together, Huw on a handsome roan mare and Belinda on a friendly little gray-and-white pony, obedient, but with just enough will of her own to make riding her a friendly partnership. Leaving the stud farm, they struck up a track on the right of the valley and soon began to mount the steeply rising slope. The sun, low in the sky now, was directly behind them, throwing their shadows dramatically on the short-cropped turf.

"Your grandmother seemed very well," Belinda ventured to break the stretching silence.

"As always," Huw replied shortly. Then, after a brief hesitation, he said musingly, "The question is, should I be trying to persuade her to go into some kind of home for old people?"

Belinda looked at him in surprise. "Are you considering it, then?"

"I was asking your opinion," he said with a shrug.

Warily Belinda began, "Your grandmother appears to be amazingly capable for her age, even with her blindness. I'd imagine that she would prefer to carry on living here and looking after you. She seemed very content to me."

"Indeed she is," Huw said fervently. "Gran and I are extremely close—which is only natural, of course, considering that she brought me up from when I was a child."

"Then why are you thinking about a home for her?"

Huw reined in his mare abruptly, turning her to look back across the valley. Jasmin followed suit of her own accord.

"It's a most peculiar thing," he began slowly in his lilting Welsh voice, "that scarcely a month ago Mrs. Barbara Lloyd gave it very forcibly as her opinion that I was a fool to lumber myself with my blind old grandmother. Yet here you are today giving me precisely the opposite advice."

Belinda felt a chasm opening before her. She was learning new, unpleasant aspects of Barbara's character every hour.

"Well, I guess I've changed my mind," she floundered. "I mean . . . after seeing this morning how well your grandmother copes with everything."

To Belinda's relief Huw merely nodded and dropped the subject. As they rode on, returning the way they had come, the sun was edging lower in the western sky, with a line of shadow creeping down the opposite flank of the valley. Below them the farm looked very neat and orderly, with its white-painted fences and well-maintained buildings. Drifts of smoke from the chimneys lay on the still winter air in a faint blue haze.

"You and Jasmin go well together," he commented after a few moments.

"She's a doll!" Belinda said impulsively, leaning forward to pat the mare's neck.

"Yet you told me once," he continued, "that Jasmin was too staid and stolid for words. You always liked Keffel better. Another change of mind?"

"I . . . I guess so." Belinda turned away to conceal the color that was creeping to her cheeks. Far below them a tractor hauling a loaded hay wagon chattered its busy way from the huge Dutch barn, obviously carrying feed for the night to the loose boxes.

Huw said abruptly, "D'you see the falcon hovering over Moelglas?"

Belinda glanced at him quickly to see which direction he was looking. But instead she met the full, head-on force of his gaze. In confusion she turned away again, feverishly scanning the sky above the hilltops for a sign of the bird.

"You don't know where to look, do you?" Huw commented in a triumphant voice.

"I . . . I don't know what you mean."

"Oh, but I think you do!" His eyes accused her. "You've been darned clever, I grant you that, but too many things have been out of character. You seemed to me so changed from the way Barbara had always been before. So changed for the better, I might add. I just couldn't make you out. And I was really puzzled this morning when the dogs raced up to greet you like that, wagging their tails. Then Apollo accepted you quite calmly, without any sign of being resentful. Even with all that, though, I still didn't suspect anything. The likeness is so extraordinary that you fooled me completely. It took the inner sight of an old blind lady to see through to the truth. I thought my grandmother was crazy when she asked me again who you were after you left us this morning. 'It was Mrs. Lloyd, Gran, as you perfectly well know,' I said. But she'd have none of it. 'If the woman who sat in that chair drinking our tea looked like Mrs. Lloyd,' she insisted, 'then it must have been that twin sister of hers we've heard about.'"

Belinda sat as if frozen in her saddle, unable to utter a sound. After a few moments' silence Huw remarked, "You don't attempt to deny it, I notice."

"How . . . how can I deny it?" she asked huskily.

"How can you, indeed? So I think that you'd better start giving me an explanation, Belinda . . . Vaughn, isn't it?"

She nodded wretchedly, staring down at her pony's white mane. "I suppose you'll tell Adam?"

"That depends on what I hear from you," Huw said grimly. "So start talking, Miss Vaughn. Just exactly what has happened to your sister?"

Belinda raised her head and met his challenging eyes. "Barbara is somewhere in the Far East. I don't know quite where."

"The Far East! What the devil is she doing there?"

Stumblingly Belinda started to explain, endeavoring not to make her twin sound too utterly callous and unfeeling. "I . . . I'm sure she wouldn't have run off with another man like that if she'd known about Adam's accident."

"No?" Huw's tone was deeply skeptical. "That would make it even more likely, I'd have said. I can't imagine *her* doing the Florence Nightingale bit. She'd have found it all too boring for words. Anyway," he went on, "you still haven't explained why you're pretending to be Barbara. You surely weren't imagining that you could just step into your twin sister's shoes and carry on for the rest of your life as Adam's wife?"

"Of course not!" she protested, flushing scarlet.

"So what is it exactly that you're doing here, Belinda?"

Her mouth was dry and her throat felt tight. "I tried my best to persuade Barbara that if she was dead set on leaving Adam the very least she could do was to call him and explain things. But I couldn't get her to agree. It seemed awful to me that he shouldn't be told. And I guessed that if she didn't arrive home on Saturday evening as expected Adam would get straight on the phone to me asking what had happened to her. So it would be up to *me* to tell him anyway. I had this crazy feeling that it might be easier—not quite so impossibly difficult, I mean—if I broke the news to him face to face. In fact, it was Barbara's own idea that I should come to Wales, but at first I wouldn't even consider it. Then when she went off, leaving her return ticket in my apartment . . . well, it seemed to make sense for me to use it. But when I got off the train I heard about Adam's accident."

Belinda looked at Huw, pleading for his understanding. Even she herself found it difficult to understand how each step had led so inexorably to another. "It was a taxi driver who told me," she went on. "He called me Mrs. Lloyd and said he'd take me straight to the hospital. I was so shocked to hear about Adam that I didn't attempt to explain that he'd made a mistake about who I was. It was all too complicated. Then, when I got to the hospital, Adam himself mistook me for Barbara. And he looked so pleased to see me, Huw, so overjoyed. It was obvious that he was in a very bad way, and . . . well, I just couldn't bring myself to tell him the truth just then and explain why I had come. It seemed the kindest thing while he was still in such a state of shock not to disillusion him."

Huw was silent for several moments, then he let out a long sigh. "Yes, I can see it was a very difficult situation," he said slowly. "But for heaven's sake . . . you *still* haven't told him! Why have you let it go on and on?"

"I didn't intend to," Belinda said pleadingly. "You must believe me, Huw. I meant to tell him just as soon as possible and return to London on Sunday as planned. But that was before I had an interview with the doctor. Dr. Llewelyn warned me—thinking that I was Barbara, of course—that when Adam was discharged his recovery would depend a lot on me. I had to see that he had plenty of rest. I was terrified then of what the shock of finding out about Barbara might do to him. So I've just had to let things ride from day to day," she finished unhappily.

Huw nodded, seeming uncertain. "But how long d'you think you'll need to keep it up?"

"I suppose another few days. Adam's getting better all the time and it's just a matter of breaking it to him gently. Except now that you've found out I suppose I've got to tell him right away—or *you* will!" Belinda felt a sudden flurry of panic at the thought of what this might do to Adam and she looked at Huw beseechingly. "Please . . . will you give me a chance to pick the best moment? If I promise to tell Adam the truth sometime in the next forty-eight hours, say, will you remain silent until then?"

Huw passed his hand across his face in a tired gesture. "What a wretched business it all is. It's going to be a terrible blow to Adam. Even though it was obvious to everyone that things between him and Barbara weren't working out as he'd hoped they would, Adam never seemed to stop loving her. He kept on trying to make the marriage work. And now . . ." Huw broke off, then added slowly, "All in all, I reckon that perhaps you'd better go on with your original plan and leave telling him until he's a bit stronger."

Relief surged through her. "You mean that you won't give me away?"

"For the moment, no. But I'm not promising for how long, mind."

"And what about your grandmother? Will she tell someone what she suspects?"

Huw shook his head. "Gran isn't a tittle-tattle."

"But I suppose you'll tell her? I mean, confirm what she's already guessed."

"I will. But that will be as far as it goes . . . for the present."

"Thank you, Huw," she said warmly. "I'm really grateful."

He looked at her with grave eyes. "Perhaps I'm being a fool, agreeing to carry on with this madness," he remarked musingly. "But I've got a feeling that I can trust you, Belinda. I reckon that you're doing this for Adam's sake. So you can count on me."

"Thanks, Huw," she said again. "I can't tell you what a relief it is to have someone on my side. Someone who won't seem like an enemy just waiting every minute to trip me up."

Chapter Five

"By the way, darling," Adam said, slipping an arm around her waist, "what about Belinda?"

Again it shook her, hearing her own name spoken by Adam. "What . . . what do you mean?" she stammered. She had just finished his evening massage and Adam was looking far more relaxed, his torn shoulder muscles obviously causing him less pain than before.

"You've scarcely mentioned her name since you got home," he explained. "I suppose her big romance fell through? Like all the others?"

"Her big romance?" she repeated dazedly.

"That chap in New York you told me about. The one who was so crazy about her, who she kept playing up. Cliff Something-or-other, wasn't it?"

Belinda's mind whirled, trying to make sense of this. "Cliff Willis, you mean?"

"That's right. I take it, considering that she's come to London for a twelvemonth, that it's all off between them?"

"It was never really on."

Adam turned to look at her in surprise. "But you told me they were as good as engaged." He gave a shrugging little laugh in which there was a note of bitterness. "Belinda didn't act one bit on that Swiss holiday like a girl who had an understanding with a chap back home. If you hadn't put me wise, Barbie, I'd never have guessed that she was such a terrible flirt."

Belinda felt a crawling sense of dismay, and with it the beginnings of rage against her twin sister. She wanted to demand an explanation from Adam, to insist that he "remind her" of exactly what "she" had said to him. But that would be much too dangerous a thing to do.

"You must have gotten it wrong," she said with an attempt at lightness. "Cliff Willis was never important to Belinda."

"No? Well, he obviously thought he was, poor chap. I suppose she just ditched him like all the others you told me about?"

"Are you sure that's what I said?" she stammered. "I don't remember it quite like that."

"Well, I do," replied Adam. "I remember very well, because I found it so difficult to believe it of her. No wonder you were so reluctant to tell me, darling. It must have been very painful for you, knowing that your twin sister could treat men so casually, without any regard for their feelings."

Belinda knew, without a doubt, that it had been a deliberate act of sabotage on Barbara's part. Her sister had taken pains to wreck her burgeoning romance with Adam by a subtle injection of poison. No other explanation was needed now for his sudden cooling off toward her and for the way he'd switched all his attention to Barbara herself. Adam must have formed a very low opinion of the girl who, while virtually engaged to one man back home in New York, was encouraging another man to get serious about her. Cliff Willis had been just a colleague at Orbital Travel in New York. It was true that they'd dated a few times, but never seriously! And she hadn't given Cliff the slightest reason to think that he might become important to her. Barbara herself hadn't actually met Cliff—or anyone else at Orbital, come to that—so Barbara couldn't have misread the situation.

And there wasn't a single thing she could do about it, Belinda agonized, to put the record straight. Even if Adam had asked her straight out in Switzerland she probably wouldn't have stood much chance. She could hardly deny Cliff Willis' existence, and it would have been difficult to convince Adam that he meant nothing whatever to her. Barbara had done her work with skill.

Yet now, after only ten months of marriage, Barbara had thrown away her stolen prize. One day, one day soon, Adam would have to find out that his wife had deserted him for another man. What, then? Was it possible that once Adam was disillusioned about Barbara he might turn again to the sister he had first been attracted to? It was much more likely, Belinda thought with gnawing despair, that he would reject them both in his disgust, regarding the Vaughn twins as despicable birds of a feather.

The next morning, shortly after ten o'clock, Belinda left the house and went looking for Huw. Seeing her from his office window, he came out into the yard to meet her.

"How's Adam this morning?" he asked.

"Restless. Inactivity doesn't suit him."

"I can guess!" Huw glanced around to make sure

they couldn't be overheard. "It's just as well for you to keep out of Adam's way as much as possible, Belinda. Less risk."

"He more or less pushed me outside," she said ruefully. "I think he imagines that I'll be bored with just his company."

Huw regarded her steadily. "Barbara would have been!"

"I told Adam I'd come and make myself useful," she explained.

"Hardly in character! Your sister exercised the ponies as and when she felt in the mood. And then only on mounts she fancied, which were not necessarily the ones we needed ridden. Apart from that she never did a thing to help."

"Well, I'm not Barbara . . ."

"But you're supposed to be!" Huw reminded her sharply. "So you'd better not start being too helpful and willing. Such uncharacteristic behavior from Mrs. Lloyd would stick out like a sore thumb." He lifted his tweed cap and raked stubby fingers through his black hair. "It really beats me how Adam ever fell for that one."

Belinda knew the answer to that now. But she couldn't bring herself to tell Huw. It was just too painful.

"He's very much in love with my sister, isn't he?" she asked thoughtfully. "Even when Adam is a bit stronger it's going to be a terrible shock for him to learn what Barbara has done."

"I'm afraid he'll blame himself," said Huw, frowning.

"Why should he?" Belinda demanded, though it was precisely what she herself had guessed he'd do.

"Adam is a completely straightforward and honest man," said Huw. "So much so that he could never imagine the woman he'd chosen as his wife could be anything but the same. So he'll reason that if Barbara found life with him intolerable it must be *his* fault, not hers. You'll see that I'm right."

Belinda felt overwhelmed with despair. "Will he try to get her to come back to him?"

"Who can say?" Huw spread his hands expressively. *"Would* Barbara come back, do you think, if he went chasing after her?"

"I don't know. Only if it suited her to."

Huw regarded her for a moment in silence, then he asked gruffly, "You're in love with Adam, aren't you?"

Belinda gave him a startled, frightened look. Were her feelings really so transparent? For her pride's sake she tried to stammer a denial, but the words wouldn't come.

"That's how you got yourself involved in this mess, isn't it?" continued Huw, nodding as if only now did the situation really make sense to him. "That's why you bothered to come to Wales in the first place, so as to try and break the news gently. You couldn't bear to think of him being hurt, could you? And when you found he was in hospital and he mistook you for Barbara . . . you just hadn't the heart to disillusion him. I thought it was a kind of guilt over what your twin sister had done or something. But I see now that it was love."

Belinda blinked to hold back tears. "I've loved Adam," she confessed brokenly, "from even before Barbara met him."

Huw pried a stone from the yard with the toe of his boot and kicked it savagely away. "I'd better tell you a bit more about how this stud is run. The only reason you've got away with complete ignorance so far is that Barbara took no interest. But even Barbara couldn't avoid having a few bits of know-how rub off on her. So try to look suitably bored talking to your husband's stud groom, as she would have done, and I'll explain what's what."

Some of the things Huw told her Belinda did in fact already know, from the time in Switzerland when Adam himself had talked so enthusiastically and she had listened so enthralled. Without drawing attention by pointing, Huw identified for her the various mares in the nearby paddocks—animals whose names Barbara would certainly have known. Most of them were carrying foals that would be born in the spring, at the right time to benefit most from the kinder weather and the rich, new-growing pasturage. These Welsh ponies were delightful creatures, intelligent and full of zest, with fine-shaped heads and bold, wide-set eyes, their sturdy native qualities having been reinforced over the centuries by judicious matings with the Arab strain. All the ponies at Glyn-y-Fflur at present, Huw explained, were the stud's own stock: brood mares, plus yearlings and two-year-olds from previous seasons that would in due course be sold as young riding ponies. Soon a number of visiting mares would be arriving to give birth to their foals and shortly afterward, when they were at their most fertile, they would be put to one or other of Adam's two prize stallions, Apollo and Splendid. These visiting mares would spend several weeks at Glyn-y-Fflur before they were returned to their owners certified as being in foal once more.

Belinda had previously noticed a number of cattle grazing in several of the paddocks along with the ponies, but she hadn't dared to display her ignorance by asking about them. Now she could.

"Horses are always very bad grazers," Huw explained. "For no apparent reason they concentrate on various patches of grass and ignore the rest, so the paddocks soon become 'horse-sick.' Cattle solve this problem. They're not selective feeders like the ponies and they clean up a paddock in no time. Or sweeten it, as we say."

"So you need to be farmers, too?" said Belinda with a smile.

"At Glyn-y-Fflur we do, on account of being so isolated here. We run our own small dairy herd, which is looked after mainly by Gwillam Phillips. But if we had neighboring farmers we'd probably find it simpler to rent out the grazing rights. That's what most stud farms do."

They did a quick tour of the various buildings: the stallions' quarters and the ranges of loose boxes where the in-foal mares were brought in at night during this coldest part of the year. Belinda saw the spacious covering yard where mare and stallion were brought together at the proper time, the foaling sheds and a whole range of storage buildings. Each time they encountered one of the hands Huw helpfully whispered his name into Belinda's ear. No doubt the men thought it strange that the boss's wife should suddenly be displaying so much interest in things, but she guessed it could be passed off as an unwelcome necessity because of Adam's present condition.

After finishing the rounds Huw strolled with her toward the house. A small blue car was approaching along the track and it drew up beside them. The driver was Elspeth Davies, the hospital physiotherapist.

"Good morning, Mrs. Lloyd," she said as she got out. "How's your husband getting on?"

"Oh, Adam's making marvelous progress."

"That's good news! I thought I'd better pop over to make sure that you were treating him gently enough." She turned to Huw with a warm smile. "And how is the knee, Mr. Morgan?"

"It's fine, thank you, Miss Davies."

Her glance lingered on him for a moment before she turned back to Belinda. "Mr. Morgan had a nasty wrench when one of the ponies kicked him. I put him on deep-heat treatment. That was before your time, of course. He seems to have managed to keep out of trouble since."

There was a friendly, teasing note in Elspeth's voice. She could become very fond of Huw, Belinda decided, but he seemed entirely unaware of her interest. Men could be so blind! Blind to the sterling qualities of one woman, just as they could be blind to the flaws of another.

After chatting for a minute or two Huw excused himself and went back to work. Elspeth watched him go with regret in her eyes.

"Huw Morgan is a nice man," Belinda commented as a feeler.

"Yes, isn't he." Elspeth became brisk. "I'd better get inside and see the patient, I suppose."

In a sheltered little dell behind the house Belinda had found some early celandines, their vivid yellow cups glowing bravely in the January cold. Frosty though it remained, a soft golden haze of sunshine lay over the valley each day from dawn to dusk and the nights were clear and bright with stars.

On Friday morning there was a visit from the local doctor, whom Adam unwittingly identified for Belinda when they heard his booming voice in the hall as Megan let him in.

"It's Evan Gruffydd, darling! I suppose he wants to run his stethoscope over me." As the door opened and Megan announced the visitor Adam called, "Hallo, Evan! Come along in."

"From the sound of you, Adam, you're as fit as a flea!" Evan Gruffydd was a short, dark, bouncy sort of man, with wavy hair that he kept flicking back from his forehead. The glance he awarded Belinda held a certain reserve. "How are *you*, Barbara?"

"Oh, fine . . . Evan."

He nodded and opened his black bag. "Now, let's have a look at this man of yours. Another three months laid up, will he be?"

"Three months?" she gasped in dismay.

"Evan's little joke," said Adam. "You ought to know his warped sense of humor by now, darling."

In fact Adam was pronounced to be making excellent progress.

"What did I tell you, darling?" he asked triumphantly, and to Evan he went on, "She's been fussing over me like a mother hen, making me rest all the time and refusing to allow me to do a single thing for myself."

"Quite right, too." The doctor flicked Belinda a glance of surprised approval. "Rest, rest and then more rest is what you need, Adam. The reason you *are* doing so well is that you've had someone taking such good care of you. So see that he obeys orders, Barbara, and we'll have him properly fit in no time."

"But I can't stay stuck here in the house," Adam objected. "For pity's sake, Evan, I've got to be allowed a *look* round outside, at least."

The doctor rubbed his chin thoughtfully. "Just a short tour in the car, then . . . half an hour at the most. Take it very gently, Barbara, and see that he's well wrapped up."

"Like some geriatric case!" Adam grumbled.

"Like a sensible man who understands that he's had a serious fall and that his body needs a chance to recover. A strong chap like you, Adam, can work himself to the limit and no harm done when he's a hundred percent fit—as you usually are. But at present you really do have to take care."

"Oh, very well," he agreed resentfully.

His first tour, Adam insisted, had to be that very day. In fact, it was all Belinda could do to persuade him to wait until after lunch. She felt very thankful to have had the session of coaching from Huw. With any luck she now knew enough about things not to make a stupid mistake and give herself away.

Belinda fetched the car from the garage, glad of the chance of a few moments in it alone to familiarize herself with the controls. At least, she reflected as she steered it round to the front steps to collect Adam, she wouldn't for the moment be called upon to drive on public roads where she'd need to remember to keep to the left. To Barbara that was something that would be second nature by now.

Their first stop was at Huw's office. He came out when he spotted the car and leaned in at the window that Adam had wound down.

"This is unexpected," he greeted them, giving Belinda a questioning look from under his brows.

"The doctor said it would be okay," she told him.

"And not before time!" growled Adam. "How're things, Huw?"

"No problems." He mentioned a phone call he'd had from a pony-trekking club in the Brecon Beacons about some additional mares they'd be needing this summer. "Oh, and Rowella has a bit of a chill. I'm keeping her inside, of course, but it's not enough to call the vet for."

Adam nodded. "And Apollo?"

"Trying to look innocent, as if butter wouldn't melt in his mouth."

Adam laughed. "We'll go and have a word with that fellow."

Belinda drove on between the fenced paddocks, stopping when they reached the one where the black stallion was placidly cropping grass together with three mares who were all in foal by him. Hearing the car, Apollo raised his fine head, ears pricked.

"Come on, then," Adam shouted.

The stallion pointedly looked away. He resumed

grazing, but always moving slowly in their direction, his mares following at a little distance.

"He's a proud one!" said Adam, admiration in his voice. "I know he's not your favorite horse, darling."

"He's beautiful!" she protested instinctively.

"Say that to *him*"—Adam laughed—"and he won't be able to resist you. He loves flattery. Come on, then, old chap!"

Apollo hesitated, then dropped all his feigned resistance. With a nicker of pleasure he came to them at a canter, his black mane flowing. He stood by the paddock fence, his head reaching toward Adam's outstretched hand, which he pretended to bite, receiving a friendly smack on the nose in return.

"You're a villain, aren't you?" said Adam fondly. "But you won't catch me out again like that, I warn you!"

Belinda could see that there was real affection between the man and the stallion, and she was very thankful that their relationship hadn't been soured by Adam's fall. It would have been terribly sad if the splendid horse had been held to blame for something that was really all her sister's fault. Getting out of the car, she walked round to pet and fondle the mares, who had come to stand at the rail, too.

"I'm glad you feel able to take more interest now, darling," said Adam. "It always seemed to me that if only you could begin to give your heart to this place there's so much you'd come to enjoy about it. Horses are fascinating creatures."

"I know," she said huskily.

Adam smiled, looking pleased. "I remember Belinda telling me in Switzerland how you two girls lived almost entirely for horses when you were children."

Belinda closed her eyes against this poignant reminder of those wonderful days when feelings of love and longing had flared so swiftly between herself and Adam. He would still love her now, she thought chokily—as her *true* self, not as his imagined wife—had not Barbara intervened. She herself had continued to love Adam unceasingly. She loved him now with a desperate yearning that could never hope to find fulfillment. How perfect her life would be if Adam had married her instead of Barbara and brought her to this beautiful valley of his, to work in partnership with him among his ponies. As it was, the beauty all around her roused a bitter pain in Belinda's heart.

"When Belinda comes to stay," Adam went on, "you two will be able to go riding together again, won't you? It'll be quite like old times for you. I'm so glad that you'll be able to see her regularly, darling."

Belinda felt like saying that she wouldn't care if she never set eyes on her twin sister ever again. That the special tug of affinity between them was broken irreparably as far as she was concerned. "We . . . we don't need to be together all that often," she replied cautiously. "I mean, if we see too much of each other, we tend to disagree."

"I know," said Adam with a sympathetic smile. "It's a pity that Belinda is always so ready to pick quarrels with you."

Belinda almost gasped out loud. What a lot of poison Barbara must have injected into his mind against her. Why, for heaven's sake? Could it be that she'd wanted to ensure that Adam never let his thoughts dwell kindly upon the twin sister who'd been the first one of them to spark his interest?

After his evening massage Adam insisted on eating in the dining room again. The outing this afternoon had brought more color to his lean-featured face and to Belinda he looked wonderfully handsome. As their glances locked across the table Adam gave her a happy, loving smile that made her heart lurch with painful joy.

Megan, who was daily becoming less hostile toward her, brought in an appetizing-looking dish of veal cooked in a cream sauce, served with savory rice and broccoli spears. It seemed to Belinda that now that Megan's cooking was no longer being criticized all the time she was making a special effort to produce something rather more exotic than her usual plain home cooking.

"That looks really delicious, Megan," she said sincerely.

In reply Belinda received a pleased, if somewhat anxious smile. "I hope I got it right, Mrs. Lloyd."

"Oh, I'm sure you have." Belinda picked up her fork and took a morsel of veal from the serving dish. "Mmm! Absolutely perfect!"

Adam remarked thoughtfully, "I wish you wouldn't stand on ceremony with my wife, Megan, after all this time. The name's Barbara . . . right, darling?"

"Of course!"

"Well, if that's the way you want it . . ." But Megan sounded slightly doubtful, as if wondering how long this out-of-character affability would last. Yet what else could she have done but agree to Adam's suggestion? Belinda thought confusedly. She was supposed to be Barbara, yet she was constantly finding it impossible to behave as she instinctively knew that Barbara would have done.

Belinda agreed to Adam having wine with his dinner this evening, but stipulated that he should limit it to just one glass. When, with a grin of rueful resignation, he went to fill her own glass she shook her head. Surprised, Adam commented, "Come to think of it, until this evening I haven't seen you have a single drink since you got back from London."

"I wouldn't enjoy drinking alone," Belinda said, hoping this was the best answer.

"You never let it bother you before." At once his hand went up in an apologetic gesture. "Sorry, I shouldn't have said that, Barbie. What's past is all behind us now, and it's the present and future that count." He smiled at her fondly. "Right, darling?"

Belinda nodded, covering her confused lack of response by helping herself to some more of the chocolate mousse Megan had made for dessert.

When they'd finished eating Adam suggested going through to the drawing room, saying, "It'll make a change of scene for me."

"But shouldn't you get to bed now?" she asked anxiously. "You've been up a long time today."

"No, darling, I feel fine. Absolutely great!" He grinned at her. "Of course, I'd go to bed like a shot if you'd come with me. But as it is I'll settle for cuddling you on the sofa."

Belinda cast him a nervous glance. "Be sensible, Adam!"

"I *am* being sensible. Up till now I've contained my impatience, but I'm already twice the man I was when I came out of hospital."

"All the more reason for not risking any setbacks."

"Have a heart! Do you seriously expect me to keep my hands off you, darling, when you float around looking more tantalizingly desirable than ever before? I may have a few odd torn muscles and so on here and there, but I'm just as much a susceptible male as I ever was—as you'd very soon discover if you didn't spend most of the time hovering way out of reach. Come here and let me prove it!"

Belinda, her heart thudding wildly, remained sitting at the table. "For heaven's sake, Adam . . . Megan will be in any moment."

"And you imagine that she'd be scandalized to catch us kissing? Never mind, you little puritan, Megan will have gone home in a few minutes and then we'll have the house to ourselves."

"Adam," she protested with jumping nerves, "I really think you ought to go straight to bed."

"No chance!" he responded. "And it'll be your fault, Barbie, for looking so beautiful and sexy."

Belinda felt a flurry of fear. Had the moment come when she must tell Adam the truth? If he was so much better this evening, surely he could withstand the shock of learning that his wife had deserted him? But while her mind argued this way, her heart was saying something quite different. Apart from the ordeal of confessing to Adam, she felt a curious reluctance to take any step that would bring her stay at Glyn-y-Fflur to an end. For all the dangers of this role she was playing, for all the anxiety about being caught out, she knew that these past few days had been more precious to her than any period before in her whole life—with the sole exception of the brief time in Switzerland when she had believed that Adam was falling in love with her.

So again Belinda postponed the inevitable moment of truth. Another day or two . . . until after the weekend, perhaps? Just so long as she didn't bring this strange, bittersweet interlude to a close quite yet.

The drawing room was already warm from the central heating, but Megan had slipped in to put a match to the pine logs in the hearth, so that a cheerful blaze greeted Adam and Belinda as they went in. The coffee things were set on a low table before the huge, feather-cushioned green velvet sofa.

"Let's not have any lights on, darling," Adam suggested as he limped through the doorway with the aid of a cane. "It's perfect with just the fire-light." Though he gave a little sigh of relief as he sank down onto the sofa after his exertion the lines of strain on his face were completely absent now. "Come and sit beside me, darling," he urged her, smiling.

"I'll just pour the coffee, and—"

"You can pour the coffee from here," he pointed out. "And after that, I forbid you to do another thing all evening. I want to keep you within kissing range."

Adam sat with his arm loosely across Belinda's shoulders while she attended to the coffee. Sipping it, making the small cup last as long as she could, she stared fixedly into the blazing heart of the fire.

"Why so pensive, darling?" he asked after a while in a softly caressing voice.

Ignoring his question, Belinda burst out in a panic, "Adam, I really think you ought to go to bed now."

"I agree," he said to her surprise, then added, "But not downstairs! I lie here thinking of you in that big double bed of ours, wanting desperately to be up there with you, Barbie darling. You can't deny that I've been very good so far, but there is a limit to what a man can stand. So tonight I'm coming upstairs."

"You are not!" Belinda said, aghast.

"Give me one good reason why not."

"Because . . . Well, you know the reason, Adam. You're simply not fit . . ."

"I'll show you whether I'm fit or not," he countered.

Belinda started to get up, to move away from him,

but Adam's grip tightened at once—with a strength that alarmed her.

"Please," she begged, not wanting to struggle too much in case she caused him some harm. "Don't act like this, Adam."

"For pity's sake, how is a husband supposed to act with a wife he's crazy about?"

"But . . . but you're not in a fit state at the moment. It could be dangerous."

"It does me a darn sight more damage," he argued, "to have to lie back and watch you all day long. This hands-off policy you've adopted is torture for me, darling . . . can't you understand that?"

"But it's for your own good, Adam," she protested, still struggling as much as she dared.

"I'll show you what's for my own good! Something more on these lines."

Belinda gasped in dismay as his mouth came down on hers in a hard, passionate kiss, his tongue thrusting in to curl sweetly against hers. Desperately, as a fierce longing for him surged within her, she fought to escape. But to no avail. With a smothered laugh of triumph Adam pushed her down and rolled himself over to cover her, crushing her into the soft cushions with the weight of his hard male body. His lips left hers to trace a trail of tender passion across her cheeks, her brow, imprinting a gentle kiss on each of her eyelids and brushing against the silky auburn tresses of her hair.

"Oh, Barbie," he murmured huskily. "You're so beautiful. I've never wanted you so much as these past few days. Ever since you walked into my room at the hospital I've been just counting the hours until I could really hold you in my arms again, really kiss you, really make love to you. The waiting has been agony, darling. You can't deny me now."

At this moment there was nothing in the world

Belinda wanted more than for Adam to make love to her. Never before had she experienced such a sweet, tormenting sense of longing as that which pervaded her whole body. Her will to resist him was fast ebbing away and Belinda clung to it desperately. It was the bitterest irony that, although she loved this man with her whole heart and soul, loved him so much that she was ready and willing to give herself to him utterly, it was something she must on no account do—for Adam's own sake! What hatred he would feel for her afterward, what disgust against himself, were he to discover that he had made love to another woman in the mistaken belief that she was his wife.

So Belinda fought a frantic battle against her own fevered longing. Whatever happened, she must not succumb, she *must not*. Somehow or other she had to get through this night without committing that final folly. With a superhuman effort she kept her body still and unresponsive. Against every screaming instinct, she remained a limp deadweight in Adam's arms. He kissed her again, almost savagely, trying to arouse her to passion. His hands roamed her body, sliding over the warm curves of her flesh, then coming up to her breasts, holding them cupped through the fabric of her dress and caressing until she felt she would cry out from the rapture of it.

Yet still Belinda fought to remain motionless and unresponsive, and in the end she won, though it was a victory devoid of any sense of triumph. At long last, breathing heavily, Adam too became still.

"What's the matter, Barbie?" he demanded, his voice deep with reproach. "Why are you acting like this?"

"You know why," Belinda responded tonelessly.

"I don't! Can't you see that you're driving me out of my mind? A man can only stand so much."

"Adam, be sensible!"

"Sensible! For pity's sake, Barbie," he groaned. "I know that this side of our life, like everything else, has tended to go sour on us in recent months. But now, just when I thought you and I were all set to make a wonderful new beginning, you have to turn cold on me."

"It's not that at all," Belinda protested in a faint whisper.

"You could have fooled me," he retorted bitterly. "Just for a minute tonight you were everything I ever hoped and dreamed of . . . warm and loving and passionate. And then . . . wham! You froze like a block of ice. Except that even a block of ice does melt in the end, and you didn't seem to."

"Adam," she stammered unhappily, "please try to understand . . . it's very hard for me, too."

"Is it, darling?" His anger was instantly gone and he touched her cheek with his fingertips in a tender gesture. "I love you so much and I want to think that you love me in return."

Belinda's heart was thudding painfully and her throat felt tight with emotion. Adam, as if suddenly doubtful, said urgently, "You do love me, darling, don't you? Say you do!"

It was so easy to say it. Madness, of course, but so easy! "I love you, Adam," she murmured huskily. "I love you very deeply." In all this tangled web of deceit, that was the one great shining truth.

Adam gave a long sigh of satisfaction, as if a question that was torturing him had at last been answered.

"Then for heaven's sake stop this nonsense," he said with a gentle smile. "Two people who are in love as we are should spend their nights together. To be separated is a crime against the precious gift of love. I'm not just talking about passion, darling. I'm talking about lying in bed with you soft and warm in my arms . . . waking in the morning to find you there beside me."

"Don't talk like that!" Belinda choked. "It's not fair."

"And are *you* being fair to me? How much sleep do you think I'll get tonight if I have to spend it in that bed down here, thinking of you upstairs? Wanting you so much."

"Do you imagine that I'll sleep any better?" she cried, feeling a curious sort of bitterness against Adam for pressuring her so unbearably.

He threw her a look of pained bewilderment. "These past few days I've been overjoyed because it seemed that at last things were going to be really good between us . . . that we were in tune as never before. Surely you realize how much it would mean to me to sleep with you again? And yet you stubbornly refuse."

"But the doctors said . . ." she began miserably.

Adam made an impatient gesture with his hand. "Do you expect me to get a medical certificate declaring that I'm fit to go to bed with my wife?"

"I don't care what you say," she choked out desperately, "you can't make me change my mind. It's *you* I'm thinking of, Adam . . . only you. Please believe that."

The dark eyes, so hard and bitter with angry frustration, melted to gentleness. "Just tell me this, darling . . . do you want me as much as I want you?"

"Yes, oh, yes," she said passionately, and quite truthfully.

His fierce grip relaxed a little. He touched his lips to her forehead, murmuring, "That's the most important thing, darling, knowing that you love me. Knowing that you want me. Okay, then, I'll accept your harsh ruling. I'll contain my impatience as best I can . . . for the moment! But it's not going to be easy, seeing you around all the time looking so desirable. I'll be counting the hours, Barbie!"

Chapter Six

The phone rang while Belinda and Adam were having breakfast. Megan was upstairs cleaning, so Belinda went to answer it.

"Hallo. Glyn-y-Fflur Stud Farm."

"Hi, sweetheart!" It was unmistakably the smooth, self-confident voice of Dorian Pettifer. "I was hoping you'd be the one to answer the phone."

"What do you want?" she asked nervously, thankful that she'd shut the dining-room door as she came out.

"That's not a very nice way to talk to your lover," he reproved her. "I think I've been extremely patient so far, Barbie, waiting for you to get in touch. But my patience has run out, sweetheart. I think you'd better come over here sometime today."

"But I can't possibly do that," Belinda objected. "How could I leave Adam?"

"Don't try and make me believe you've stayed home acting the comforting companion ever since he came out of hospital. I know you better than that. Besides, I spotted you out riding with the stud groom."

"You *saw* me?"

"I was walking along the top ridge and I had my binoculars with me. You two seemed to be having a very absorbing conversation. Have you suddenly taken a fancy to him or something? You've always been so contemptuous before."

"We were talking . . . business."

"Business, eh? How interesting! I'd have thought the office was the place for talking business, not halfway up the hillside well out of earshot of other people."

"If you imagine there's anything between Huw and me you must be crazy," she said hotly.

"Listen, Barbie, I don't care whether there is or isn't. If you want to amuse yourself with the hired help go right ahead." The lightness left his voice. "Only don't let it interfere with you and me. So what time shall I expect to see you?"

"I can't come," Belinda reiterated. "How could I?"

"With the greatest of ease. Take one of those nice long rides of yours. I should think Keffel would know the way blindfolded by now. I'll find a few apples for her as a treat."

"I'm not coming," she said desperately. "It . . . it has to end between you and me, Dorian."

"Barbie," he said warningly, "be sensible and don't make me angry, or I might do something you'd be sorry for. So which is it to be, this morning or this afternoon?"

Belinda's thoughts raced in panic. Obviously it wouldn't do Dorian any good to carry out his blackmail threat to tell Adam that he and Barbara had been having an affair. But she didn't want to risk the chance of him acting out of spite. Very soon now Adam was going to have to face the terrible shock of learning that the wife he had loved so much had left him for another man. It would add immeasurably to his pain to learn that even while still living at Glyn-y-Fflur she had been blatantly unfaithful to him. If, Belinda argued, she appealed to Dorian Pettifer's better nature—in the role of Barbara, of course—then surely there was a chance he would listen. It was worth a try, at least. By agreeing to see him she had nothing to lose.

She came to a firm decision. This morning Huw was coming to talk about various matters with Adam, which meant that she'd be free up until lunchtime.

"Listen," she said into the phone, "I'll be with you around eleven. We'll talk about things then."

"What is there to *talk* about, sweetheart?" He chuckled. "Okay, see you!"

Belinda took several slow, steadying breaths before returning to the dining room. Adam glanced up from reading a horse-breeding journal that the postman had delivered just that morning.

"Who was it on the phone, darling?"

She couldn't bring herself to tell him a complete lie. "It was Dorian Pettifer," she said, trying to sound casual.

"What did he want?"

"Oh, he was inquiring about you, and . . ."

"That was decent of him. Did you make noises about him coming for dinner sometime?"

"Not really. I . . . I thought we'd leave that for a while."

"Okay, darling, that's your department." To her relief he changed the subject. "According to an article here, the market for top-quality Welsh ponies is on the up and up. I'm sure you won't complain, Barbie, when you see even bigger profits rolling in."

"Adam!" Belinda was gripped by a sudden impulse to blurt out her confession to him right here and now. To get it over and done with.

"What is it, darling?" he asked.

Belinda stared back at him unhappily. "I . . . I've got something to tell you." Then her throat seemed to close up and she couldn't continue.

Adam reached out across the table for her hand, holding it tightly while he studied her face. "Come on, out with it, darling," he coaxed. "It's not like you to be shy." Suddenly his expression changed, his dark eyes sparking with joy. "You don't mean . . . you're not trying to tell me that I'm to be a father?"

Horrified at this dreadful misunderstanding, Belinda jerked her hand away. "No!" she cried loudly. "No, it isn't that!"

"Don't be upset," he soothed. "That was a foolish thing for me to think. It was just . . . well, the way you looked, so concerned and serious about my reaction, I thought perhaps . . ." He smiled at her. "I know that we agreed to wait awhile for that, but it's more your wish to delay than mine, and as far as I'm concerned we can have a baby just as soon as you like. Anyway, setting all that aside, darling, what is it you have to tell me?"

Her heart thudding wildly, Belinda stammered, "It's terribly difficult to say, Adam. I don't know where to begin. You see . . ." Dear heaven, where could she find the right words?

"Whatever it is, Barbie, remember that I love you. So come on, darling, what's this all about?"

"Will you . . . will you promise to hear me out without getting angry?"

"I promise," he agreed slowly, but she could tell from the look in his eyes that he was seriously concerned about her.

Belinda took a deep breath. "The fact is, Adam, that I'm not really . . ."

At that moment the door opened and Megan came in to clear away the breakfast things. As they waited for her to be gone, making an effort to chat normally while she stacked the dishes on a tray, Belinda realized what a fool she'd been to embark on such a difficult explanation with a third person in the house. The instant Megan departed for the kitchen she became brisk, insisting that it was time for Adam's massage. He made several attempts to get her to finish what she had started to say, but Belinda firmly shook her head.

"We'll talk about it this evening," she said finally, and it was a commitment as much to herself as to Adam.

This time Belinda rode Keffel. She was a lovely golden color with a black mane and tail, one of the larger class of Welsh pony, standing at some fourteen hands. Though well-behaved, she was not docile, but full of mettle and game for anything. And as Dorian had forecast, once on the path to Tyfawr Cottage she seemed to know the way without guidance.

It was a heavy, overcast morning, with a rawness in the air that matched Belinda's somber mood. She dreaded the meeting ahead and felt less hopeful with every passing moment that it would achieve anything.

Topping the final rise, she reined Keffel in and glanced back. The stud farm could no longer be seen because of a jutting shoulder of rock. So that was why Barbara had so often been able to leave the valley without anyone noticing!

Sighing for her sister, Belinda started on the last stage of her secretive journey. After about a quarter of a mile she spotted a chimney from which a thread of white smoke curled up toward the leaden sky. Soon it was revealed as belonging to a sturdy cottage, stone-walled and slate-roofed, with a patch of unkempt garden surrounding it. Through the open doors of a timber garage she could see Dorian's yellow sports car.

Giving Keffel her head, Belinda arrived at the cottage five minutes later. As she drew near she wondered where Barbara would normally have left the mare. Fortunately, that problem was solved by Dorian, who came out at that minute and called to her, "Take Keffel round to the back as usual. I've left the door open for you."

The door he referred to proved to belong to a large wooden shed. True to his word, Dorian had provided a couple of apples for Keffel to munch while she waited, together with some hay and a bucket of clean water. He had followed Belinda round and watched as she dismounted and led the mare into the makeshift stable.

"You're exactly the right antidote for a miserable day like this, Barbie," he remarked. "I had a complete mental block this morning and I couldn't write a thing. So I phoned you."

"I wish you hadn't," Belinda said. "Suppose Adam had answered?"

"I'd have been discreet, darling. How is he now, anyway?"

"Getting better fast."

Dorian nodded indifferently, putting his arm about her shoulders as they walked round to the cottage door. This opened directly onto a large square room, with a low-beamed ceiling and a stone-flagged floor strewn with bright rugs. Inside, with the door closed, Dorian swung her round to face him and drew her into his arms. But Belinda put up both hands, her palms against his chest, and thrust herself back from him.

"No, don't do that," she said tersely.

"What d'you mean, don't do that?" he demanded, looking astonished. "This is what you've come for, isn't it?"

"No, I . . . I came because we've got to talk, Dorian."

"There are times," he said reproachfully, "when talking is a waste of a golden opportunity. We don't have all that long, sweetheart. I suppose you've got to be back home for lunch?"

"Of course."

"So stop being silly! Off with that anorak and come and sit by the fire."

It was warm in the room from a large wood-burning stove, so Belinda allowed him to take her parka. After tossing it onto a chair Dorian caught her in his arms again before she could move away, holding her pressed close against him.

"You're a sensation in jeans, you little witch," he muttered, his lips against her hair. "Which is exactly why you put them on."

Belinda struggled wildly in his imprisoning arms. "Dorian, just stop this! I told you, I've come here to talk. There are things you've got to understand."

He chuckled disbelievingly. "What is the game, Barbie? You always were a tease, weren't you? I remember how you played hard-to-get that first time, just to pique my interest. And then . . . you suddenly took off like a rocket. All systems go!"

"I'm not playing any kind of a game," Belinda protested vehemently. "You forced me to come, Dorian, with your threats."

"Come off it!" He laughed. "You came because you wanted to, sweetheart."

Stifling her further protests, he claimed her mouth in a hard, possessive kiss, trying to force her lips open with his probing tongue. Relentlessly he pressed her backward, until Belinda fell onto the sofa that was drawn up before the stove and Dorian came down on top of her. He was a powerful, muscular man, and she realized to her horror that there was little she could do to fight him off.

After threshing about helplessly for a few moments, she brought her hand up and gave him a stinging slap on the cheek.

"You little vixen!" he cried, jerking back from her. "You meant that, didn't you?"

"Of course I meant it! If you'd only listen, instead of . . . of . . ." Belinda scrambled to her feet and pulled down her sweater. She had an urge to grab up her jacket and rush out through the door. But to what avail? She still hadn't achieved her purpose in coming here this morning: to make Dorian understand once and for all that his affair with Adam Lloyd's wife was at an end. How much easier, she thought desperately, if she could only tell him the whole story. So long as Dorian believed her to be Barbara it was almost understandable that he refused to believe that she was being serious.

"What the devil's got into you?" he muttered angrily. "You've never been vicious like that before."

"I . . . I had to be, to stop you."

"Okay, so now you've stopped me! Quite a passion killer, a slap in the face like that. You'd better do some explaining."

Nervously Belinda moved farther away from him, unaware that against the glow of the open stove her shapely figure was clearly outlined and her hair blazed in a halo of rich copper-gold. "Dorian, just because there was something between us once, it doesn't mean that things will go on in the same way forever."

"Agreed," he said. "But there has to be a good reason for bringing it to an end."

Somehow the words and phrases Belinda had

rehearsed on the way here wouldn't come out right. "A . . . a love affair, well, sometimes it runs out of steam without there being any particular reason," she faltered.

"Ours hasn't run out of steam for me," he said, frowning. "And I'd take a bet it hasn't for you, either. A woman like you, Barbie, whose husband is, shall we say, temporarily incapacitated, must be feeling sick with frustration. So just exactly what's going on?" His vivid blue eyes narrowed swiftly. "Is it that stud groom? Have you started something with him?"

"Huw? Don't be crazy!"

"Well, it's got to be somebody, knowing you! And stuck here in Wales, who else is available?"

"There doesn't have to be anybody," she snapped. "Adam needs me right now and I refuse to . . . to cheat on him."

Dorian regarded her steadily, assessingly, as if trying to work out the reason for her sudden change of heart. "Listen, I've been thinking lately . . . you and I are really good together, so maybe we should make things a bit more permanent. You could hang around here for a while until Adam is fit again, if that's going to salve your conscience. Then we'll be off and away. Okay?"

Belinda glared at him furiously. "Of course it's not okay!"

"Don't get so shirty," he returned, shrugging his shoulders. "I was only making a suggestion. I thought that maybe it was what you were hankering after."

"Well, you're wrong," she said hotly.

"Think it over for a few days," he advised. "You may find you like the idea, after all. And in the meantime, there's no reason why we shouldn't enjoy ourselves the way we've done before." He moved toward her purposefully and Belinda backed away in alarm.

"Dorian, please be sensible," she begged, realizing with a pang that these were the selfsame words that she had used to Adam last night. To both men, in their different ways, her behavior must seem beyond understanding. She had managed to convince Adam that it was for the sake of his health that she had refused to let him make love to her. But what convincing reason could she offer Dorian Pettifer for a similar refusal? "Listen," she ran on feverishly. "Isn't it better to finish while we're still good friends, Dorian?"

His handsome face was dark with anger. "Just like that, on a sudden whim of yours! What the devil d'you think I've come to Wales for, Barbie, right in the middle of winter? Okay, it's true that I've got some scripts to write and I need peace and quiet, which I can never find in London. But I also need something by way of diversion . . . what man doesn't? And I was counting on you. Surely I had a right to, after what we've been to each other the last few times I was here?"

"I'm sorry," Belinda said wretchedly, lost for any new line of argument that might move him. "You've just got to believe me when I say that it's all over between us, Dorian."

"And if I don't?" he snarled. "I could make a lot of trouble for you, Barbie . . . with Adam."

Though Belinda was trembling in every limb, she faced up to him squarely. "I'm aware of that, Dorian. But what good would it do you—except to make me end up hating you? Besides, I'm sure you don't really wish Adam any harm. He's been really ill, you know; that fall was a terrible shock to his system."

Abruptly Dorian's anger faded and he gave a

shrugging laugh. "You've got a nerve, Barbie, pleading so prettily on your husband's behalf! Aren't I even going to get something to remember you by? A consolation prize, you might say."

"No, Dorian, not even a consolation prize."

"If that's how it's got to be, that's how it's got to be!" He tilted his head and looked at her. "I'll be staying here for about another week, I reckon, so if you should change your mind . . ."

"I won't."

"You never know. Anyway, have some coffee before you venture out in the cold again."

Belinda only wanted to be gone now. But as she herself had pointed out, it was better for them to part friends. So she agreed and a few minutes later she sat with Dorian before the roaring stove, drinking coffee. As soon as possible, however, she put down her cup and rose to leave.

"A parting kiss?" Dorian suggested. "Just to show there's no hard feelings."

Belinda was about to refuse. But after all, she had won, so what did a mere kiss matter? When she lifted her face to his Dorian caught hold of her eagerly. His kiss was fierce and passionate and Belinda felt a deep sense of repulsion; it was all she could do not to break away forcibly. But she steeled herself to allow the kiss to continue. When at last Dorian let go of her he smiled ruefully.

"I thought I might be able to melt you," he said. "Still, if you should change your mind, sweetheart, I'll be here for a while longer."

"I won't change my mind," Belinda said, and picked up her parka.

Dorian helped her on with it, his hands lingering a little at her shoulders. "I still think you might. I'll be waiting, and hoping."

Riding away, turning before she passed from view

of the cottage to give Dorian a final wave, Belinda felt strangely cheerful, even though the sky was heavy with storm clouds. It was as if, by winning this one victory, she had solved all her problems. But the biggest problem she'd ever had to face in the whole of her life lay ahead of her this very evening. She had made a definite promise to Adam—and to herself— and there was no dodging it.

Keffel picked her surefooted way down the sloping flank of the valley. When they reached a point from which the stud farm became visible Belinda loosened the reins and allowed Keffel to nibble the short turf while she looked down at the cluster of buildings. Glyn-y-Fflur beckoned her with a painful nostalgia. Above every other place in the whole wide world it was where she would always long to be. But her stay here had come to an end.

Having left Keffel with young Davy to unsaddle, Belinda made her way back to the house. Adam must have spotted her returning, for when she went in, he was standing waiting in the doorway of his temporary bedroom, leaning heavily on a cane. Then, to her dismay, she saw that his face was twisted with rage. Had he found out where she had been that morning?

"Come in here!" he ordered curtly.

Silent and afraid, she obeyed. Adam shut the door and stood facing her.

"I've just had a phone call . . . from London!" he grated.

Belinda felt helplessly transfixed by the piercing anger in his eyes. Her mind raced frantically. Had her boss somehow managed to trace her sister's address in Wales and called her here? But even so, what could Adam have pieced together from that?

"Ph-phone call?" she stammered. "Who from?"

"From my wife!" he stated.

"But . . . I don't understand." Her voice came out as a faint whisper.

"You mean you don't understand how she came to be in London? Actually, Barbara called me from the airport. She'd just flown in from Hong Kong. So I'm afraid, Belinda, that your deception is at an end. Now it's time for some explanations. And they'd better be good!"

"What did Barbara tell you?" she faltered.

"Never mind what Barbara told me; that's between the two of us. I want to know what you thought you were up to, playing this absurd practical joke on me. What the devil did you hope to achieve by it?"

"It wasn't a joke, Adam," she stammered wretchedly. "I . . . I only did what I thought was best."

"Best for whom?" he demanded harshly.

"For *you,* of course!" At this there was a contemptuous snort from Adam and Belinda rushed on. "Please listen . . . you must believe me. I didn't plan any of this; it just happened. I came to Wales in the first place to break the news about Barbara leaving you and going abroad. It seemed the best thing to do—I mean, it wouldn't have been easy to give you bad news like that over the phone. Then when I got here I learned from the taxi driver at the station that you'd had this accident. He mistook me for Barbara, you see, and so did the receptionist at the hospital, and it all seemed too complicated to explain to them that I *wasn't* your wife without revealing the whole story. And then you thought I was Barbara, too, and you seemed terribly glad to see me, and . . . and considering what a bad state you were in I was afraid to disillusion you. To make matters even worse, when Dr. Llewelyn sent for me he said you were insisting on being discharged and he was relying on me to see that you kept calm and didn't overdo things. So what was I to do?" she finished pleadingly. "I decided that I'd have to keep it up for a little while, until you were stronger."

"And then?" The terse question was rapped out. "You couldn't have imagined such a deception could continue for long, for heaven's sake?"

"No, of course not," Belinda said miserably. "I was just going on from day to day until I felt you were well enough. I got leave of absence from my job, and . . ."

"I know you did! After Barbara's call I phoned Orbital Travel, hoping to make some kind of sense of the situation. The switchboard girl informed me that you were away from work because of a family crisis . . . something to do with your brother-in-law, she believed. I didn't tell her who I was, of course."

"Th-thank you . . ." she stammered.

"Don't thank me. I did it for my own sake, not yours! I'm not going to let this story leak out. I'd be a laughingstock all around the district."

"I'll leave right away," Belinda offered wretchedly. "This very minute. Huw will drive me to the station, and . . ."

"Are you out of your mind? What exactly would you tell Huw?"

Belinda tried to discipline her spinning thoughts. She mustn't reveal to Adam that his stud groom knew the truth already. He'd be even more furious. Huw had kept silent only because she'd begged him to and it wouldn't be fair to get him in deep trouble with his boss.

"I . . . I wouldn't need to tell Huw anything," she said. "I mean, it's going to get out sooner or later that Barbara has left you, Adam, but people don't need to be told that in fact she never came back after her trip to London . . ."

"Barbara *is* coming back," he clipped. "She's on her way right this minute."

"Coming back?" Belinda echoed dazedly. "I don't understand."

"I don't yet know the whole story," Adam admitted. "She said it was all very complicated and she'll explain when she gets home. Poor darling, she was very upset. I know that a lot of what's happened is *my* fault, not hers. I've not been as sympathetic as I might have been and things just got too much for her, so she took off without considering the consequences. It's in her nature to act impetuously without thinking things through." His eyes hardened as they came to rest on Belinda's face. "Not like her sister! You seem to have behaved in this business with cool calculation all along the line, though heaven knows what you hoped to achieve in the end. You're a very mixed-up sort of person, Belinda, and you need to get yourself straightened out."

Belinda's eyes flooded with tears at this bitterly unfair charge. For a moment or two Adam hesitated, looking uncertain, but then he continued brutally. "It's no use turning on the waterworks with me, Belinda. I realize that you must be a past mistress of that art. How many men have you used the trick against, I wonder?"

Adam's lips curled in an expression of contempt. He took a couple of limping strides toward her and stood looking down at her with narrowed eyes. Belinda felt herself trembling as he stood so close, not quite touching, his vital male warmth seeming to bridge the gap between them.

"It's astonishing," he said, "how two sisters can look so exactly alike and yet be so totally different in character. One so honest and straightforward—hot-headed sometimes, yes, but basically sincere—and the other so complex and full of guile. What makes

122

you like that, Belinda? Does it give you a sense of power to manipulate men, to play games with them? When I think of the way you led me on in Switzerland, making me believe that you were really sincere about me! And now you come here posing as Barbie, amusing yourself by watching me make a complete idiot of myself."

"No!" she cried vehemently. "You've got it all wrong, Adam. Wrong from start to finish."

"Are you trying to tell me there wasn't any man named Cliff Willis?" he challenged.

Belinda bit her lip. "There was, but he didn't mean anything to me."

Adam pounced on her ill-chosen words. "Exactly, Belinda! No man ever does mean anything to a woman like you."

"You do!" she jerked out.

"Huh! It'll take a lot to convince me of that," Adam retorted bitterly.

What was the use of protesting that she loved him and had almost from the day they first met? Belinda thought despondently. She dreaded the look of scornful disbelief she would see in his dark eyes if she made such a claim. She said in a low, choked voice, "There's no point in us talking, Adam; you'd never believe anything I said. Just tell me when I can leave and I'll get out of your life."

"How easy you make it sound," he sneered. "We'll have to wait till Barbara gets here and talk about the best way out of this sorry mess. Needless to say, she's absolutely furious about it."

"Barbie knows?"

"Of course she knows! I could hardly have avoided telling her, even if I'd wanted to, considering that when she called me I was so taken aback that I gabbled out that it couldn't be Barbie I was talking to because my wife was right here at Glyn-y-Fflur.

For a moment I had a crazy idea that it must be you on the phone from London, Belinda, playing some stupid practical joke on me. But when she finally convinced me that she really was Barbie there was only one answer to who *you* were. You're going to have a lot of explaining to do when your sister gets here. A *lot* of explaining!"

Belinda felt a surge of bitterness. "Hasn't *she* got a lot of explaining to do, as well?"

"I told you, that's between the two of us. You don't come into it, Belinda."

"Just so long as you get at the truth," she returned.

"The truth! Would you even recognize the truth if it hit you between the eyes? I doubt it!"

She looked at Adam's face, set stone-hard against her. She could never, she thought in an agony of misery, hope to get through to him. Barbara had poisoned his mind against her forever. Even after deserting him for another man she still had such a hold on Adam that she would come back to him and be accepted joyfully.

With a heavy sigh of defeated resignation Belinda asked, "What are we going to do, Adam? Have you worked out a plan?"

He nodded and said in a flat, unemotional voice, "You'll have to go to the station and meet Barbie. I can't drive yet, and we daren't send anyone else. On the way back you can explain to Barbie exactly how things stand—and tell her I reckon it's best for you to work a switch over and return to Glyn-y-Fflur as yourselves. We'll concoct a story for the benefit of the staff here that Barbara's twin sister is paying us a flying visit. Tomorrow, or maybe it had better be the day after tomorrow, you return to London. And that will be that."

Belinda nodded listlessly. "You must love Barbara very much," she whispered.

"I do." Adam seemed about to attack her again, but he quickly got himself under control and merely said brusquely, "Now you and I will have lunch together as if nothing has happened and we'll tell Megan that your sister is coming to visit, so will she please prepare a room for her."

Chapter Seven

Winter dusk was already falling as Belinda set out to meet her sister. When she reached the highest point of the one and only road out of Glyn-y-Fflur tiny snowflakes were whirling in the headlights. Despite having the heater turned on full blast, a sense of raw chill invaded the car and Belinda couldn't help shivering.

She felt nervous about having to drive on the left, even knowing that there would be little or no traffic on the country roads. But far worse was her dread of the forthcoming encounter with her sister. It would be no use for Barbara to try to browbeat her, though . . . *she* was the one in the wrong and they both knew it, even if she could somehow convince Adam otherwise. And however foolish, however ill-judged her impersonation of Barbara had been, Belinda could console herself with the thought that she'd done it from the best of motives. Whatever Barbara and Adam chose to believe, she could cling to that.

There was one person on her side, though. Huw Morgan. It wasn't until Belinda went to fetch the car from the garage that she'd found a chance for a quick word with Huw.

"Barbara is coming back?" he said incredulously. "She's got a nerve! But as I said, I expect Adam will forgive her."

"It sure looks like it," Belinda agreed miserably. She quickly filled him in on Adam's plan. "I wanted to warn you, Huw. Otherwise, confronted by the two of us together, you wouldn't have known what to think."

"I reckon I'd know which of you was which," he said meaningfully. "When will you be returning to London, Belinda?"

"The day after tomorrow, I guess."

"So soon!" Huw frowned. "And I suppose you'll never be returning to Glyn-y-Fflur, after this?"

Unwittingly he had twisted a knife in Belinda's heart. She swallowed down a sudden rush of tears. "How could I ever come back now?"

"Does Adam realize that *I* know?" he queried.

"No. I managed to keep that from him. Whether he ever finds out is entirely up to you, Huw."

He nodded, letting his eyes rest on her in a long look. "It won't be the same here without you, Belinda. I wonder if Barbara will be at all changed."

"A little chastened, perhaps." Though she doubted that. Barbara was Barbara and in her mind other people existed merely for *her* convenience. Deep down Belinda had always know that, but she had only fully appreciated it during the past few days. "I'll have to get going, Huw, or I'll be late for Barbie's train."

As a matter of fact the train was late, and Belinda

had a forty-minute wait at the little country station. Fortunately the only other passenger to alight—a farmer's-wife type who gave her a nod of recognition—had trudged off into the gathering darkness before Barbara appeared.

Belinda had decided to remain sitting in the car, since she was anxious to avoid an outburst from her sister that might be overheard by other people. As Barbara came walking out she reached over and threw open the door on the passenger side. When Barbara saw who was in the driver's seat she gave a gasp of astonishment.

"What the devil . . . ?"

"Get in and shut the door," Belinda ordered crisply.

Taken aback, Barbara obeyed. But as Belinda began to drive off her sister said furiously, "You've got a nerve, talking to me like that. And you're the very last person in the world I expected to meet me. I thought you'd have had the decency to be gone by now, to be well out of the way before I arrived."

With a feeling almost of hatred Belinda said curtly, "I wanted to be gone, believe me, but Adam thought it would take too much explaining. This way we can cover up the fact that you deserted your husband and then, when it suited you, came rushing back again. Why have you come back, anyway? What's happened to your great romance with Nigel Dixon?"

"That's none of your business!"

"You've got to have some sort of story to tell Adam," Belinda pointed out in a tight voice.

"Oh, no problem there. The guy is crazy about me. He always has been." Barbara hesitated a moment; then, as if she needed to unburden herself of her seething anger, she burst out, "That Nigel was a fake! He gave me a line about what a big shot he was—a senior partner in an exporting business, he said. But he was nothing more than a sales rep. My first shock was when I discovered that we weren't flying first-class, but he spun me a tale about first-class being fully booked. Then when we got to Singapore I found that he'd taken a room in a second-rate hotel. I really blew my top, I can tell you!"

Belinda tried to suppress an unworthy feeling of triumph. "So you promptly walked out on Mr. Nigel Dixon?"

"Well, not right away. I mean, it was a bit difficult. I was stuck out there in the Far East with no funds and only my credit card. But after a couple of days I decided I'd had enough, whatever the problems, so I arranged a flight back to London."

"And immediately phoned Adam from the airport?"

"Naturally. I knew he'd be glad that I had decided to come back to him." Barbara's voice swelled with anger again as she went on. "But what a shock it was to have Adam insisting that I couldn't possibly be Barbara phoning from London, because his darling wife was there in Wales at that very moment. It took quite a while to figure out between us what must have happened. What in the name of heaven did you think you were up to, Belinda, posing as me? Surely you weren't so stupid as to imagine that you could slip into my place and live happily ever after with my husband?"

"No, of course I didn't." She drew the car to the side of the narrow roadway and pulled on the hand brake. "We've got to talk, Barbara."

"You bet we've got to talk! I want to know just how much damage I'm going to find you've done."

"Don't you want to hear about Adam's accident first?" asked Belinda bitterly. "Aren't you concerned about how seriously he was injured?"

Barbara shrugged. "Adam can't be too bad. He

sounded okay on the phone. He got thrown by Apollo, I gather."

"Just as you did! Only with far worse consequences." Belinda dearly longed to tell her sister that she knew all about the other incident with the black stallion and how Barbara had mistreated the animal in her fit of temper. But it would mean involving Huw, which she mustn't do.

"That wretched horse is a positive menace," Barbara declared. "He's vicious and Adam ought to have him put down. Or sell him. One or the other."

"There's nothing vicious about Apollo," Belinda protested heatedly. "And I'd strongly advise you not to suggest anything like that to Adam."

"I'm not such a fool, Bel. But Adam can't go on being so obsessive about his precious farm. That was the cause of most of the trouble between us, as I told you in London. It makes me so darned mad! We could be really wealthy if only he'd sell the wretched place. We could live anywhere in the world . . . think of it! I'd love to go back home to the States—California, maybe."

Belinda gasped in horrified amazement. "Is that all you can think about at a time like this? I'd have thought you'd be trying to concentrate on how you can possibly make it up to Adam for the way you walked out on him. . . ."

But Barbara, it seemed, wasn't even listening. "It really gets my goat," she went on, "to think of the fortune that Adam's got locked up in a lot of useless horseflesh. Still, I guess that I'll have to go easy. Play a waiting game."

"That's not your usual style, is it?" asked Belinda bitterly. "Normally you just rush in and grab what you want with both hands. And never mind anyone else's feelings."

"What's bugging you, Bel?" Barbara turned to face her and in the glow of the instrument panel lights Belinda could see her green-gold eyes gleaming with amusement. "Are you jealous because I've got something you'd like for yourself?"

"Meaning what?" demanded Belinda, her heart in her mouth.

"Meaning Adam! You've always wanted him, haven't you? But it's not my fault if I'm the one Adam chose."

"You lied and cheated to get him," accused Belinda before she could stop herself. "I found out from something Adam let drop that you had the nerve to tell him I was as good as engaged to Cliff Willis."

Barbara didn't even blink. "And weren't you?"

"You know I wasn't!"

"You'll be telling me next that Cliff Willis didn't exist," said Barbara with a soft laugh. "That he was just a figment of my imagination."

"You knew perfectly well that there was nothing serious between Cliff and me."

"Did I?" Barbara's eyebrows arched in derision. "Don't look so hurt and indignant, Bel. You know what they say . . . all's fair in love and war."

"*Love,* you call it!"

"Call it what you like. Okay, Bel, let's come clean . . . we both wanted the guy and I won. It's as simple as that. Adam fell in love with me in Switzerland and nothing's going to stop him being in love with me now."

"Only because he's the sort of decent, honorable man who thinks that if his marriage goes wrong it must be *his* fault."

Barbara's eyes widened. "Did he tell you that?"

"Something of the kind."

"I told you I had him hooked!" Barbara said smugly. There was a moment's thoughtful silence before she went on. "What I want to know, though, is this: precisely what have you two been getting up to these past few days? If you played the part of being me, and Adam was taken in by it, then . . ."

"Nothing happened," Belinda hastened to assure her. "You seem to forget that your husband has had a bad accident."

"A few bumps and bruises wouldn't stop a husky man like Adam for long. Especially considering that you must have been flirting with him for all you were worth."

"You're wrong!" Belinda cried furiously. "It wasn't like that at all."

Barbara gave her a long, searching look. "Are you telling me that Adam isn't capable of making love yet?"

"No! I mean . . . how should I know, for heaven's sake?"

"Let's get this straight," Barbara snapped. "Just exactly what have the sleeping arrangements been?"

"Adam has a bed downstairs in the small living room. Megan and her husband fixed it for him."

"And you?"

"I've been sleeping upstairs, in your bed."

"And Adam showed no signs of wanting to join you there?" Barbara sounded incredulous.

"Listen," Belinda said desperately, "he's got to have lots of rest and quiet. That's doctors' orders."

"I can't imagine Adam taking doctors' orders if it didn't suit him."

"I made him!"

Barbara pounced on that rash remark. "So? You're saying he *did* want to go to bed with you, but you argued him out of it! I wonder why, Bel? Did you figure that making Adam wait a bit would make him less likely to notice any little differences between us."

"You've got it all wrong," Belinda said unhappily.

"You're seriously asking me to believe that the

idea of sleeping with Adam didn't even cross your mind?"

Belinda wished that she could make a flat denial. But it wouldn't be true and she feared that a rush of color to her face would give her away. Avoiding her sister's intent gaze, she took a deep breath and said, "I realize that the situation was getting a bit . . . difficult. So I'd decided that the time had come to tell Adam the truth. Afterward I was planning to leave here right away."

"And when was this momentous confession to take place?" Barbara demanded.

"Last night," she said. "Only . . ."

"Only you didn't!"

"I did try. But it wasn't an easy thing for me to do."

"I know what *is* easy for you," Barbara mocked. "It's easy to claim *now* that you intended to tell Adam the truth. But I don't think you intended to at all. You thought that with me out of the way you could carry on as if you were his wife for as long as you wanted."

"That's crazy!" Belinda protested. "I was definitely going to tell him tonight. Can't you understand, I've only been waiting for Adam to get stronger, and . . ."

"Listen," Barbara cut in harshly, "that guy is as strong as they come and a fall from a horse wouldn't put him out of action for more than a couple of days at most. So you can cut out all this idiotic claptrap. Whatever your cunning little game was, Bel, it's all over now. So when are you leaving? Tomorrow?"

Belinda swallowed miserably. "Adam suggested the day after, to make it look more genuine that your sister is paying a visit from London."

Barbara considered this. "Maybe he's right. But get this clear, Bel . . . no tricks! Because I can beat you, every single time. Check? Now, we'd better be getting home."

"You have to take over the driving," said Belinda in a tense, controlled voice. "And we'd better trade coats. Megan will still be at the house and she might notice."

"Okay." They stepped out of the car to effect the switch. The snowflakes were whirling faster now and the road was lightly powdered with white. Belinda shivered with the cold as she took off the striking llama-trimmed coat she'd deliberately put on.

"You've been making free with my wardrobe, I see," Barbara commented as she slipped out of her coat and handed it over. To Belinda's relief it was an ordinarily styled tan raincoat, so no suspicions would be aroused if anyone remembered having seen Adam's wife wearing one just like it.

"Well, I had to, didn't I?" she replied. "I only brought one change of clothes with me from London."

Barbara shrugged her elegant shoulders into the llama-trimmed coat. "Oh, I guess so."

When they reached the narrow pass into Glyn-y-Fflur the snow was falling thickly and swirling in the wind.

"Just my filthy luck!" exclaimed Barbara self-pityingly. "I'd have thought twice about coming back here if I'd known it was going to be like this."

Belinda made no reply; her heart was too filled with bitterness and anger.

At the house they acted out a charade for the benefit of Megan, who appeared from the kitchen to greet them. Apart from their coats, they had decided to change shoes, too, and as an afterthought they'd both put on headscarves to conceal the slight differences in their hairstyles. Even so, Belinda held her breath as she was introduced to Megan. Would the woman notice anything odd? But mercifully all seemed well.

"It's astonishing," Megan exclaimed, standing back and staring from one to the other of them. "I've never in my whole life seen two people who looked so much alike."

Belinda managed a laugh, just as Barbara did, their customary reaction to people's bewilderment at seeing them together. But Adam was hardly in any mood for lightheartedness. Belinda noticed the way that he and Barbara looked at each other, obviously eager to talk, but unable for the moment to behave other than as a couple who had been parted for a mere hour or so while their visitor was fetched from the station.

"It's good to see you again, Belinda," said Adam in a cheerful voice, yet to her his tone sounded horribly forced and stilted. "Er . . . you must be cold. Barbara will show you to your room. Perhaps you'd like a nice hot bath before you change."

In other words, Belinda interpreted, stay upstairs for long enough to give Barbara and me a chance to get things sorted out. She wondered desolately what sort of story her twin would spin in order to persuade Adam to welcome her back with open arms. There wasn't a doubt in her mind that Barbara would achieve this somehow or other.

Upstairs in a guest bedroom, Belinda changed into the soft green woolen dress of her own that she'd brought to wear on her trip to Wales: luckily Megan hadn't seen her in it. Then she sat down and waited a good half-hour before descending the stairs to join her sister and brother-in-law.

Dinner was a highly uncomfortable meal. Though Barbara seemed in high spirits, Adam was withdrawn and moodily quiet. Every now and then Belinda was conscious of his gaze, charged, it seemed to her, with a burning anger and resentment.

She did her best to eat reasonable amounts of the dishes Megan had taken so much trouble to prepare in honor of her "visit," but the food seemed to choke her. When Megan brought in the coffee she made an apologetic excuse about being tired after her journey and went up to her room.

Though it was still early she undressed and got into bed. But not to sleep. She was restless, aware of the insistent patter of swirling snowflakes against the windowpanes, while she listened for other sounds in the house. At long last a door downstairs was opened, then closed. Footsteps mounted the staircase—light female steps coming alone. What had happened that Barbara and Adam were spending the night apart? Still tormented by the puzzle, Belinda at long last drifted off to sleep.

Belinda awoke early to a world of dazzling whiteness. Gazing from her window, she saw that the night's snowfall lay thick and solid, with deep drifts built up against every building. It didn't occur to her, though, to feel anything more than appreciative wonderment at the beauty of the scene, with the slanting rays of the morning sun sparking rainbow colors from the snow crystals.

Too restless to remain upstairs, she dressed and went down to face whatever had to be faced. Adam was in the hall, tapping the barometer. He looked very gloomy, but he at once put on an act of welcoming his sister-in-law so that Belinda knew that Megan must have arrived and could overhear what was being said.

"Good morning, Belinda. I hope you slept well."

"Splendidly, thanks," she lied. "This heavy snowfall was a surprise, wasn't it?"

"Yes. And it looks as if there's plenty more coming."

"Really? I hope it won't interfere with the trains,

then," she said clearly, for Megan's benefit. "It's been great coming to see you two, Adam, but I've decided I'd better not stay over a second night. I'll be leaving today."

He gave a short, unamused laugh. "You won't be leaving, you know . . . trains or no trains. Huw, my stud groom, has just been in to tell me that there's twenty feet of snow blocking the pass. Like it or not, Belinda, I'm afraid you're stuck at Glyn-y-Fflur until the thaw comes."

"Oh, no!" she gasped in horrified—and very real—dismay. "How . . . how long will that be?"

Adam shrugged his broad shoulders. "Two, three days . . . a week. Who knows?"

"But can't you dig a way out, or something?"

He laughed again. "No chance! It would take all my men their whole time to tackle a job like that. And it's quite unjustified. We're fully prepared for a short siege and we'll come to no harm."

"But I've got to get away!" Belinda cried frantically. "Surely you can understand, Adam, that I can't stay here."

He held a warning finger to his lips, then said in an affable voice, "Let's go through to my study while we talk it over." He limped in after her and firmly closed the door. His face now was rock hard as he looked at her. "You'll have to reconcile yourself to staying here, Belinda. There's no alternative."

"But it's an impossible situation," she protested.

"One entirely of your own making, I might point out." Adam paused, then went on, "We'll all of us have to get through this difficult time as best we can and I don't want you stirring up more trouble than you have done already."

"Everything I've done," she said faintly, choking back a sob, "I did for the best . . . what I thought was for the best."

"It was still unwarranted interference and I don't

want any more of it. Understand?" Impatiently Adam pushed some books aside and leaned against the desk. He didn't look directly at her as he added, "I don't want Barbie upset any more than she is already. The poor girl sobbed her heart out last night after you'd gone up to bed. I realize now what a selfish and unthinking brute I've been to her."

"You?" queried Belinda in amazement. "What makes you think that?"

"I've been too tied up with my work here on the stud farm and I've not given enough consideration to my wife's wishes and feelings. I intend to put that right in future."

"But you won't sell the stud farm?" Belinda asked, appalled.

Adam's glance flickered in surprise, then he said crisply, "There's no need for that. But I can pass over most of the responsibility to Huw and get away more." He prodded the carpet with the end of his walking stick, seeming highly embarrassed suddenly. "Obviously it's very upsetting for Barbie, knowing that you've been living here with me as my wife for these past few days. But there's no need for her to find out that I . . . that we . . ."

Belinda waited, refusing to help him out. There was a hard knot of anger in her heart. Avoiding her eyes, Adam continued, "I'm bitterly ashamed of the fact that I was fooled by your impersonation. That I . . . that I kissed you and actually wanted to make love to you. But Barbara doesn't need to know that. You *must* keep silent about it, Belinda . . . You owe us both that much, at least."

"Do you think I want to talk about it?" she retorted.

Adam hesitated a moment, then said, "I thought you might . . . use it as a weapon to hurt her with."

Belinda flinched as if he had struck her. "What a

terribly low opinion you have of me," she said huskily.

"I don't want to, Belinda, believe me! I can never forget that you're Barbie's twin sister and I'd like to be able to think well of someone so close to her. When I look at you it's incredible how alike you two are. It's almost understandable that I was so easily deceived." The expression in his eyes softened and one hand lifted tentatively toward her. "Even now . . . you look so devastatingly beautiful, Belinda. I could still so easily imagine that *you* are the woman I'm in love with."

"Don't say that," she cried brokenly. How could he, how *could* he be so insensitive? Didn't he realize the agony he was causing her?

"You've played utter havoc with my life," Adam clipped in sudden harsh accusation. "Last night . . . last night Barbie and I talked a lot and we got through to each other in a new way. I knew that all it needed to set the seal on our perfect understanding would be for us to . . ." He broke off and continued thickly, "I couldn't go through with it; I just couldn't. It . . . it was having you right here in the house, Belinda. The thought of you lying asleep in the room next to ours was just too . . . too inhibiting. I didn't explain that to Barbie, of course. She believes that I'm still obliged to sleep alone, downstairs. Which is why it's so especially important that she doesn't get to know what happened between you and me two evenings ago."

Two evenings ago she had lain in Adam's arms on the sofa and rejoiced in his passion, even while she felt compelled to resist it. Afterward she had passed a sleepless night, aware only of her blazing love for him, her desperate longing. Did Adam suppose that she'd ever want to confess all this to her sister?

"I'll never say anything," she whispered.

He looked relieved. "Thanks! This snow is a nuisance, but there's nothing to be done about it. We've just got to get through the next few days as best we can. And when you finally leave, Barbie and I can get down to the task of straightening out our marriage. We *can* do that, Belinda, and we will!"

Barbara, they learned from Megan, had ordered a breakfast tray in her room.

"I'll take it up to her," Belinda offered, seizing this chance to avoid having to eat with Adam alone in the dining room. "I only want a cup of coffee myself and I can have a nice talk with her."

"There's not a lot else you *can* do, Miss Vaughn," said Megan, gesturing at the deep snow outside. "What a pity that your visit should be spoiled like this. You'll take away such a bad impression of Glyn-y-Fflur."

"I think it's beautiful!" Belinda exclaimed unguardedly.

She received a curious look from Megan. "But you've scarcely seen anything of it, Miss Vaughn. It was dark when you arrived last night and this morning . . . well, there's little else but snow to be seen."

"I could get a view from my bedroom window," Belinda said hastily. "It looks like such a lovely, peaceful valley, cradled like this in the hills. A little world of its own."

Megan smiled her approval, then said with an undertone of criticism, "It's a pity your sister can't see it like that. She finds it all a bit too isolated for her taste."

Barbara was lounging in bed against the pillows, flipping through a glossy magazine, a transistor radio tuned to a pop station.

"Trying to make yourself useful, are you?" she greeted Belinda ungraciously. "I suppose you might

140

as well; there's nothing else to do in this awful place. Just look at that ghastly snow."

Belinda set down the tray, which aside from coffee held a glass of grapefruit juice, a soft-boiled egg, toast and butter and marmalade. "I thought this would give us a chance to talk, Barbara."

"Talk? I imagined that we'd said all there was to say yesterday, Bel. I don't much care for postmortems. Which train are you catching today? Or is it still tomorrow you're going?"

"That's one of the things we've got to discuss. The point is, I can't leave right away. Glyn-y-Fflur is snowed in."

Barbara stared, her eyebrows arched questioningly. "Don't be stupid. How can we be snowed in?"

"Adam says there is a twenty-foot drift blocking the pass. It's impossible to get a vehicle out."

"But there's got to be a way! You can't stay here. What about the mountain rescue service? They've got helicopters."

"Yes, but I'm sure they'll be reserved for emergency use only. Besides," Belinda pointed out logically, "to make such a big issue of getting your sister away from Glyn-y-Fflur would only draw attention to us, which you can hardly want. Believe me, Barbie, I'm every bit as eager to get away as you are to have me gone and I'll be off as soon as it's possible. But right now I can't leave, so we'll just have to make the best of things."

"What a terrible mess! Adam was talking again last night about us going skiing as soon as he's fit—a kind of anniversary of when we met—but I expect I'll have had quite enough of snow by then. I guess I'll talk him into taking a month in the sun instead . . . the Greek islands, maybe, or North Africa." She lazily picked up her juice and sipped it, considering the possibilities.

"Barbie . . ." Belinda hesitated a moment, then

plunged in. "Barbie, you really will try to make a go of your marriage this time, won't you? I mean, Adam is a marvelous person and he loves you very much. Everything could be just perfect for you if only you'd make a real effort."

Barbara regarded her with amusement. "You sure think a lot of the guy, don't you? You're such a romantic, Bel, that I guess you'll never learn about men. They all have their drawbacks. And let me tell you, drawbacks can be pretty deadly when you're married to them."

"But you never really tried to make things work for you and Adam," Belinda said miserably. "Even here, right on your own doorstep, there was Dorian Pettifer."

Barbara sat bolt upright at that. "Hey! Who's been telling you things?"

"Nobody. I got it from Dorian himself."

"Dorian is *here?* At his cottage?"

Belinda nodded. "But it's okay, Barbie, you don't even need to try and get in touch with him. You see, I rode over there yesterday morning and I made it clear to him that it was all finished between the two of you."

"You did *what?* Are you saying that you explained to Dorian about me going away? Told him who you really were?"

"No, he believed that I was you, just like Adam did. First I ran into him at the Black Swan Hotel, where I was staying while Adam was in the hospital. Then a few days later he came visiting here at Glyn-y-Fflur. He kept pressing me to go to his cottage and in the end he said that if I didn't go he'd tell Adam about your relationship with him. Barbie, I just can't understand how you ever got yourself involved like that with Dorian Pettifer."

Her sister made an impatient, dismissive gesture. "I guess that's where you must have been when I called yesterday morning. Adam said you'd gone out riding."

"That's right," Belinda confirmed. "Dorian called at breakfast time and luckily I happened to be the one to answer the phone. I figured that the best thing was to ride over there and have it out with him once and for all."

"What happened?" demanded Barbara. "Did you and he . . . ?"

"Did we what?" Then her sister's meaning crashed down on her and she burst out indignantly, "Of course not! What on earth do you take me for?"

Barbara gave a shrugging laugh. "I don't see why not. It's a pity, really; it would have been rather intriguing, Dorian thinking that you were me. On the other hand, maybe it's just as well you were too squeamish. You don't have my experience, I guess, when it comes to men and he'd have been sure to detect certain little differences if you'd let him get too intimate." She cracked her egg with the spoon and went on. "I don't mind admitting, Bel, I was suspicious at first when you insisted that nothing had happened between you and Adam these past few days. I couldn't see why you'd passed up the opportunity. It wasn't until bedtime last night that I realized you were serious about Adam and doctors' orders, which makes it all the nicer that Dorian is right at hand."

Belinda gasped, hardly able to believe her ears. "But I told you, Barbie," she said coldly, "as far as Dorian Pettifer is concerned, it's all over. After a lot of argument, he agreed."

"I bet he won't argue when he discovers that I've changed my mind! Dorian, my dear Bel, is a hot-blooded man. I can't wait to get over there."

"You seem to be forgetting the snow," Belinda pointed out.

"Soft snow like this will be no problem on horseback. It's just a matter of avoiding the worst drifts."

"You can't do this to Adam," Belinda burst out. "I won't let you."

"You won't let me?" her sister mocked. "Is that a threat?"

"Listen, Barbie, be reasonable . . ." she began, but Barbara cut across her words with a shake of the head.

"Being reasonable, Bel, is only another way of saying being dull."

Chapter Eight

Belinda was thankful that the blizzard, while not presenting any immediate threat to the stud farm, had left a lot of extra work in its wake. Soon after her talk with Barbara she was outside helping the men clear the piled-up snow, finding release from her pent-up emotions in the hard physical effort of shoveling. Except for those mares who were heavy with foal, the ponies were let out of their loose boxes and taken as usual to the paddocks, where hay was spread for them.

At midmorning she was surprised when Huw invited her to come to his bungalow for a cup of tea.

"Is that a good idea?" she queried. All morning he had been introducing her to the men as Barbara's twin sister from London and she'd acted as though she were meeting them for the first time.

"Why not?" Huw smiled at her wryly. "You'll be able to meet Gran as your true self. You'll receive a warmer welcome as Belinda Vaughn, I'm thinking, than you did as Barbara Lloyd."

"I'm not sure that I can face your grandmother, Huw."

"Of course you can! Gran is entirely on your side." He gave Belinda a disturbingly long look. "Just as I am!"

Sitting with Huw and his blind old grandmother round the warm fire in their big living room, Belinda found to her surprise that she was hungry. She ate three of Mrs. Morgan's delicious griddle cakes and drank two large cups of steaming tea. Huw had been right, her welcome from the old lady was extremely cordial and altogether the atmosphere was much more relaxed than on the previous occasion. No direct reference was made to the situation, but just as she and Huw were about to return to work, his grandmother felt for Belinda's arm and gripped it warmly.

"My dear, it's sorry I am that you'll be leaving us so soon," she said in her lilting Welsh voice.

"That's kind of you," said Belinda appreciatively. "I . . . I'll be sorry to leave this lovely valley."

For the sake of appearances she was obliged to return to the house for lunch. Adam, she thought, looked paler and altogether less fit than in the last couple of days, more like he'd looked when first discharged from hospital. He only toyed with the steak-and-kidney pie Megan had cooked . . . as did Belinda, her appetite having deserted her again. Bringing in the dessert of golden sponge pudding Megan frowned at the quantity they'd left.

"Didn't you like it, then? I thought something substantial would be nice on such a cold day."

"Substantial is the right word for it," Barbara

remarked acidly. "But then solid, homely fare is your specialty, isn't it, Megan?"

Ashamed of her sister's unkindness, Belinda said quickly, "I'm sorry I couldn't do justice to your steak-and-kidney pie, Mrs. Williams. It was delicious, but I'm afraid I ate too many of Mrs. Morgan's griddle cakes this morning."

Megan flashed her a surprised glance, then moved her gaze thoughtfully to Barbara. Had her suspicions been aroused? But I'm myself now, Belinda decided mutinously, and it's no good for anyone to expect me to behave out of character.

Adam was saying placatingly to Megan, "I seem to be a bit off my food today. I couldn't manage much breakfast, either, if you remember."

"You must eat, though, Adam," said Megan, mollified at once. "It's the only way to get your strength back."

He gave her a faint, apologetic smile. "I'll do my best."

As the Welsh woman left the dining room Belinda couldn't help chipping in, "Megan's right, Adam. It's most important for you to eat properly."

"Oh, leave the man alone," snapped Barbara. "He'll eat when he gets hungry." With a little moue of distaste she pushed away the dish of sponge pudding. "By the way, Adam darling, I thought I'd go riding this afternoon."

"Good idea," he said absently. "Take care, though, and avoid the drifts."

"Don't worry, I'll take care not to get caught."

From across the table Belinda met her sister's mocking gaze; it was as if Barbara was daring her to make a comment. She felt sick at heart. Within twenty-four hours of being reunited with her husband Barbara was already making plans to cheat him and there wasn't a thing she could do to prevent it.

Any attempt to warn Adam by making pointed references to Dorian Pettifer would only bring him fresh agony of mind . . . and probably result in making him hate her all the more.

She became aware of Adam's dark gaze resting on her thoughtfully. "I hope you haven't been overdoing things outside this morning, Belinda," he said, a slight furrow marking his brow. "It's good of you to help, but shoveling snow is heavy work. I only wish that I could be out there too, pulling my weight."

"For heaven's sake!" protested Barbara sharply. "You should leave such menial tasks to the hired hands. You're the boss, not a manual laborer."

Adam's eyes flickered, but he refrained from making any comment. Belinda guessed that this sort of issue was a frequent bone of contention between them.

Immediately after lunch Belinda escaped outside again. She intended to work until she was fit to drop so that she could go to bed early and sleep the sleep of exhaustion rather than spend another night lying awake, tossing and turning. But she found that there was less to do now. Huw, in his usual efficient manner, had everything organized. At the normal time, with the coming of dusk, the ponies were brought in from the paddocks and settled for the night in their loose boxes.

As Huw made a final round to check that all was well Belinda walked with him. After closing a paddock gate he stood leaning his elbows on the top rail, gazing along the valley to where the western sky above the mountains was a smoky copper-red.

"I was thinking, Belinda," he began in his slow, thoughtful way. "Maybe we could meet up in London sometime."

She glanced at him quickly, unsure exactly what he meant, but the expression in his brown eyes left no room for doubt. Huw was such a nice, kind, gentle man, she thought with a lump in her throat. She envied the woman who would one day fall in love with him. But that woman was not herself . . . not in a million years. The contempt and accusation in Adam's eyes had battered and bruised the love she felt for him, but it was not destroyed. She would go on loving Adam Lloyd even if she never saw him again. However unjustly he condemned her for what she had so misguidedly done for *his* sake, it would make no difference. Her love for him was a burning flame that would never be quenched.

"I'm sorry, Huw," she murmured, "but . . . well, I don't think that us meeting in London would be a good idea."

"Because I work here for Adam?"

She seized upon this excuse for not hurting his feelings more than was necessary. "You must see that it would make things very difficult, Huw."

"I could easily get another job," he pointed out. "Anywhere in the country. I'm not one to blow my own trumpet, Belinda, but I happen to be a first-class stud groom. There are plenty of places that would snap me up."

"I'm sure that's true," she said earnestly. "I know how much Adam values you."

"I'd be sorry to quit," Huw admitted. "Adam's been a good friend to me and I've learned a lot from him. He's a superb horse-breeder, you know, with an instinctive flair for it. And hopefully some of that has rubbed off on me. I'd hate to let him down, of course, but there are times in every man's life when he's got to think of himself first. And this is one of them!"

"Huw," she said wretchedly, "you must understand that I don't . . ."

"That you don't feel anything for me at the moment," he finished for her. "I realize that, Belinda. How could you, with things the way they are?

But as time passes, if you'd only give me a chance, I'm sure we could . . ."

"No," she said quietly and firmly. "I'm sorry, Huw, but it wouldn't be fair to let you start thinking along those lines. Besides, you have to consider your grandmother. She's settled and happy at Glyn-y-Fflur."

"I know she is," he acknowledged. "But Gran wouldn't want to think she was standing in the way of my happiness. Naturally I'd never abandon her, but I know my grandmother and she'd be ready and willing to up sticks and go wherever I went."

Belinda said thoughtfully, "I guess she'd like to see you married, wouldn't she? I mean, to some nice local girl. And there must be plenty to choose from, Huw, because you've got a lot to offer a woman. What about Elspeth Davies, for instance?"

"I know the woman I want," he said, regarding her intently.

"Honestly, Huw, I'm sure it's only because you and I have been thrown together like this." Belinda sighed inwardly and added with an attempt at lightness, "When the thaw comes and I'm able to leave here you'll soon forget me."

"I'll never forget you, Belinda," he insisted. "Never!"

As the two of them began to walk back there was a strange, dramatic beauty about the snow-mantled valley that added a poignancy to Belinda's mood of depression. The setting sun, piercing through the massed snow clouds, was shooting rays of orange fire across the landscape, burnishing the windows of the big house and the smaller dwellings. The air had a sharp nip in it and their breath hung in little clouds of vapor.

Nearing the house, Belinda stopped and looked at Huw. "I'm very sorry," she said. "Really I am.

You've been a good friend to me and I really appreciate that, but . . ."

He smiled at her in resigned understanding, then turned and walked away, his whole bearing dejected.

When Belinda went into the house Adam was standing at the hall window. Her heart faltered to see how unutterably weary he looked, despite his improved mobility.

"What was Huw so upset about?" he asked as she closed the door behind her.

"Oh . . . nothing," she stammered. "I suppose he's just tired out with so much work to do."

"I've never known work get Huw down before. He thrives on hard work normally, just as I do." Adam gave her a strange, assessing look. "It's rather a lonely life for him, stuck here with just his old grandmother for company."

"It must be," she agreed in a low voice.

"I thought maybe . . . well, you're a very beautiful girl, Belinda . . ."

Startled by Adam's shrewd appraisal of what he'd seen, she blurted out, "There's nothing between Huw and me. There couldn't be!"

"No, I suppose not." There was almost, she thought, a touch of relief in his tone. That was understandable, though. It would have been highly embarrassing for him if his senior man were to become involved with the sister-in-law Adam himself must fervently wish never to set eyes on again.

"Where's Barbie?" she asked quickly, to change the subject. She'd seen Keffel back in her loose box, so she knew that her sister had returned.

"She's having a hot bath," Adam explained. "Soaking out the aches and pains after her long ride."

Or, Belinda amended in her mind, recovering

from a long afternoon of passionate lovemaking. She was filled with disgust and wished that she hadn't mentioned Barbara's name to Adam.

She felt uneasy, embarrassed, painfully aware of the tension that was increasing by the moment as she and Adam stood looking at each other. She wanted to flee upstairs to her bedroom, where she could remain until it was time to put in a brief appearance at the dinner table. But something held her pinned there in Adam's presence. It felt almost as if there was a powerful magnetic force pulling them together.

With the last beams of sunlight snipped off by gathering clouds, the hall was suddenly darkened. Giving herself a little shake, Belinda crossed to the light switches and flicked on the shaded wall sconces. Adam's face was clearly visible to her now and she felt a shock of dismay. He looked quite haggard, his features drawn with strain, his eyes shadowed.

"What is it?" she asked in alarm. "Are you in pain?"

For several moments he regarded her with his lips set tight, then he nodded an admission. "Yes, it's not too good."

Belinda was stricken with conscience. Since yesterday, since the moment of her exposure, she had totally forgotten about massaging Adam's shoulder muscles. Obviously they had knotted up. Thinking only of bringing him relief from pain, she asked without thinking, "Shall I give you a massage, Adam?"

"How can you, now?" he retorted savagely.

"But there's no one else, Adam, and it's got to be done. I know, I'll fetch Barbara and show her how. I picked up the technique easily enough, so she should be able to as well. Then she can take over."

He looked doubtful. "I'm not sure if that would be a good idea, Belinda."

"What other solution do we have? It's got to be this way, Adam; you must see that."

After another pause he nodded reluctantly. "I suppose so."

"I'll go and tell her. Shall I help you onto the bed first?"

"No!" It was an explosive exclamation, a furious protest, and Belinda felt deeply hurt. Out of sheer necessity he would accept her hands on him while she demonstrated to Barbara. But aside from that, Adam was making it very clear that he wanted no sort of physical contact between them.

With a heavy heart Belinda turned and went upstairs. She found her sister sitting at the dressing table, applying bright-red nail polish. She was wearing a filmy georgette negligee in a pale-peach color and the perfume of bath essence hung in the air.

"Hi, Bel," was her languid greeting. "What's that solemn look on your face for?"

"Adam's shoulders are troubling him," Belinda told her in a briskly practical tone. "He has a lot of pain in the shoulder muscles."

Barbara shrugged indifferently. "Well, I guess he has to expect that. Give him a couple aspirin. Or a good stiff drink might be better."

"I've been massaging him twice a day," Belinda explained, adding hastily, "under doctors' orders. I think the sessions should be continued."

Wafting her hands delicately for the polish to dry, Barbara smiled in lazy amusement. "I bet that gave you quite a thrill!"

"It was just something that had to be done," Belinda said, keeping a hold on her temper. "The physiotherapist at the hospital showed me how and I think that I ought to show you. Will you come downstairs now?"

Barbara shook her head, seeming totally uncaring and uninterested. "I won't deprive you of your fun,

Bel. You go right ahead and massage him to your heart's content."

"But I can't do that, Barbie. For one thing, suppose Megan discovered that it was me, not you, who was massaging him?"

"She won't. Megan will be stuck in the kitchen until dinnertime, producing another one of those stodgy meals of hers."

"Please come down," Belinda begged.

Barbara shook her head again, studying her fingernails to judge the effect. "You know I've never been any good at those sort of practical things. So you just carry on for the time being, Bel, and when the thaw comes and you leave here we can call in professional help. That's by far the best way."

She should have known better than to expect Barbara to exert herself, Belinda thought bitterly, even for the sake of her husband's health. Dispiritedly she asked, "I suppose you *did* go to see Dorian Pettifer this afternoon?"

"You suppose right, sweetie."

"But you won't go on seeing him anymore, Barbie, will you?" It came out as an urgent plea, and her sister laughed contemptuously.

"You bet I will! Dorian was delighted to find that I'd 'changed my mind.' He said he never really believed that I meant what I said yesterday. It was really quite amusing, Bel, repairing the damage you'd done."

Filled with disgust and loathing, Belinda murmured huskily, "Do you really expect to pick up again with Dorian and carry on your affair just as you did before? How can you cheat on a wonderful man like Adam?"

"Because he's not quite wonderful enough, as I seem to have been telling you ad nauseam. If only Adam could realize that there's a lot more to life than breeding ponies I might feel inclined to be the faithful little wife. As it is . . . well, a girl needs a break from horseflesh now and again."

"You know what you deserve, don't you?" Belinda gasped furiously. "You deserve for Adam to find out about you and throw you out! And on top of that to discover that Dorian Pettifer doesn't want you either!"

"No chance," Barbara returned, smiling serenely. "Unlike you, I know how to handle men."

Miserably Belinda returned downstairs to Adam and put the best gloss she could on her sister's adamant refusal to massage him. "It's true that Barbie isn't very practical in some ways. . . . I mean, she's never been very good when it comes to anyone being ill and I think she's scared of doing you more harm than good."

Adam's face was a blank mask. "So that's that."

"No," said Belinda. "I'll do it. It'll be perfectly safe as long as Megan doesn't come in, because she'd know it was me from the way I'm dressed. So I'll lock the door just in case."

"But I can't expect you to massage me with things as they are, Belinda."

"Please let me," she said earnestly.

There was an oddly intense look in Adam's dark eyes as he regarded her. Belinda wondered nervously if he guessed that she loved him, wanted him, yearned for him. Massaging him would be an agony for her . . . the intimacy of laying her hands upon his naked flesh, yet never for a moment allowing her self-control to slip and reveal the depth of her emotions.

"If you really don't mind, Belinda," he murmured at last. "I feel very knotted up this evening."

"Of course I don't mind," she said with a bright, easygoing smile.

Slowly Adam unbuttoned his shirt and eased it carefully from his stiff shoulders. Stripped to the waist, he positioned himself facedown on the narrow bed and Belinda commenced her task. He lay unusually still under her ministrations, almost as if he were in a semidoze. She tried to make her mind a blank as she ran her hands in long, sweeping strokes over his rippling muscles, but she was achingly aware of his smooth warm skin, of the husky male scent of him. She found herself tracing the indented line of his spine with her fingertips, which wasn't part of the routine, and at one point she felt a sudden, almost overpowering urge to bend and press her lips to where his crisp dark hair curled into the nape of his neck. This was torture . . . torture because she knew that, unlike all the other times, the session had to end with her just straightening up and stepping back from him while Adam redonned his shirt. Performing the final strokes, she found herself wishing with a fevered longing . . . If only Adam would turn and pull her down to him, holding her in his arms and kissing her with all the passion of those other times. If only, if only . . .

Suddenly, incredibly, her dream became reality when Adam rolled over onto his back and reached out for her. With a shuddering groan he drew her closer until their lips were pressed together in a long, drowning kiss. Her body, resistant at first with surprise, became soft and pliant under his passionate embrace and she melted her full length on the bed beside him. As the kiss continued, Adam's tongue stabbed into her willing mouth exploringly and she felt his body quicken with desire as he pulled her still closer. . . .

And then, as suddenly as it had happened, it was over. Belinda didn't know afterward whether she had ended the embrace, or Adam—or both of them together—but she found herself stumbling to her feet, her cheeks hot and scarlet. Adam pushed himself into a sitting position and gazed at her in shamed apology. But even at that embarrassing moment the lamplight striking the muscled contours of his chest made Belinda gasp aloud and she quickly averted her face lest he read the naked longing there.

"I'm sorry, Belinda," he muttered. "I didn't mean that to happen. It was crazy, madness, a despicable way for me to behave. It was just . . . Oh, I can't explain. . . ."

Her voice choked, Belinda said in a whisper, "I was to blame too, Adam. I let it happen. But I've been so wretched and miserable because I thought you hated me. . . ."

"I don't hate you, Belinda," he protested, his tone suddenly gentler. "I'm not even angry with you anymore. I *should* be, for the havoc you've caused in my life, but I believe now that you meant no harm by it. Still, we mustn't risk this sort of thing happening again. We mustn't let ourselves be alone anymore until this snow clears and you can finally leave Glyn-y-Fflur."

Belinda nodded in bleak misery and turned to the door. It wouldn't open, though, and she remembered that she had locked it against the possibility of Megan intruding. Hot with new embarrassment, she turned the key and slipped outside. From the kitchen came the sound of an electric blender. Hastily, silently, she mounted the stairs and went to her room. Throwing herself down on the bed, she sobbed her heart out in a welter of grief and desolation. The future that lay ahead of her—a future without Adam—was a long, black tunnel of despair.

Dinner was an even worse ordeal than she'd anticipated. Adam sat morosely at the head of the table, his face dark and gloomy. Barbara, though, was in a curious state of suppressed excitement and she seemed to go out of her way to goad them both . . . and Megan, too. When the housekeeper placed a silver platter on the table and removed the cover to reveal a temptingly displayed roast duck surrounded by green peas and glazed carrots Barbara gave an ironic laugh.

"Quite *cordon-bleu,* aren't we? What's to follow, I wonder? Suet pudding?"

Megan compressed her lips and said nothing, obviously deeply hurt. Adam shot a pleading look at Barbara and when Megan had left the room he said reproachfully, "Go easy on her, darling. She does pretty well for us, I think. We can't expect sophisticated continental cookery from a Welsh countrywoman."

"For heaven's sake, can't I make a little joke?" Barbara laughed, pouting sulkily. She pushed her long-stemmed glass toward Adam. "Pour me some more wine, darling. I'm parched!"

Adam did so, then started to carve the duck. Obviously wanting to change the subject, he said, "There's more snow forecast for tonight. I heard it on the radio."

"Oh, no!" groaned Barbara, directing him a frowning look. "Will there be much?"

Adam shrugged gloomily. "I hope not. The men —and Belinda—have already worked like Trojans clearing snow and I don't want them to have any more to cope with while I'm out of action like this."

Barbara's mood of suppressed excitement seemed suddenly to evaporate and she grew edgy. She's thinking, Belinda brooded, that if the snow gets much deeper she won't be able to ride over to see Dorian Pettifer tomorrow. The thought gave Belinda a certain malicious satisfaction.

As on the previous evening, Belinda made an excuse and went straight upstairs after dinner. Physically tired by the day's exertions—and emotionally exhausted, too—she undressed and climbed into bed, falling at once into a heavy sleep.

She awoke to a deep night silence. Even the wind had dropped and there seemed to be a strange breathless quality of waiting . . . the calm, perhaps, before the next onslaught of snow. In the darkness Belinda rose and felt her way across to the window. When she drew back the heavy drapes she was startled by the flood of moonlight that slanted into the room.

The scene that greeted her was one of magical beauty. The snow glistened silver-white beneath the bright canopy of stars. In the entire valley, from one hillside to the other and to the farthest end, there was no movement except for the slow curl of chimney smoke. Even the winter-bare branches of the trees were perfectly still. The sudden whinny of a pony drew her gaze to the block of buildings where the livestock, horses and cattle alike, were sheltered against the freezing cold. Belinda felt her heart expand in wonder at the serene peace of Glyn-y-Fflur and she stood gazing out for long minutes, her breath misting on the windowpane.

Then abruptly the feeling of wonder was gone as harsh reality came crashing through to her consciousness. She turned to get back into bed, her heart now like a great stone boulder that weighed her down. The fleecy covers no longer seemed cozily warm and she lay there shivering miserably. Sleep, when it came at last, was a merciful numbing of the senses.

By dawn the blizzard had struck again. Awakened early by the howling of the wind, Belinda lay listening to it while she watched the daylight strengthen around the edges of the drapes. Vaguely she seemed to be aware of sounds about the house: voices down below, footsteps on the stairs. Then a sharp rapping on her door.

"Belinda, are you awake?" It was Adam's voice, tense with anxiety.

"Yes, coming." She rose quickly, drew on a robe and padded to the door. "What is it, Adam?"

He looked past her into the room. "Barbie's not with you, by any chance, is she?"

"Barbie? Of course not! Why should you imagine . . . ?"

"She's gone," he rapped.

"Gone? I . . . I don't understand."

"She's not in her room. And another thing . . . Huw's come to tell me that Keffel is missing from her loose box."

Belinda stared at him in consternation. "You mean that Barbie must have taken her?"

"Well, someone did. Keffel's saddle is missing, too." Adam spread his hands in a gesture of helpless bewilderment. "I'm desperately worried, Belinda. If Barbie had one of her madcap ideas—you know what she's like—and decided to go for a ride in the moonlight she'll have got caught in the blizzard."

Belinda's hands flew to her face. "Oh, no!"

"I can't think of any other explanation. Nobody has seen her and we've looked everywhere. There's not a sign of her."

"What will you do?" Belinda asked chokily. "Call the police, the mountain rescue team?"

"I only wish I could, but the blizzard must have brought the lines down somewhere. The phones are dead. I'll have to send one of the men to try to find a way through on horseback over the hills. Meanwhile, we must organize search parties ourselves."

"Yes, of course. I'll get dressed at once."

Adam frowned. "I don't think you should go,

Belinda. It could be dangerous; you don't know the terrain."

"I'll be okay if I'm with someone else," she insisted. "I can't stay here, worrying myself sick, when I could be out there doing something to help."

Adam considered a moment, his face creased in anxious thought. Then he nodded. "Okay, you'd better come with me."

"But, Adam," she cried, aghast, "*you* can't possibly go outside, not in your condition."

"I'm going," he stated flatly. "Do you imagine I could stay home and wait while people are out there searching for my wife?"

"But your injuries . . ."

"I'll manage! We'll meet downstairs in a few minutes. Right?"

Belinda stood and watched as he descended the staircase, quickly, but still with a pronounced limp, leaning heavily on the banister rail. She felt as anxious about Adam himself as about her sister. How could he withstand the rigors of an outdoor search in these conditions? The wind seemed to be rising rather than diminishing and through the landing window she could now see only a white curtain of driving snow. It was sheer madness for him to leave the house in this. And yet she knew with devastating certainty that nothing she could say or do would dissuade him from going to the rescue of the woman he loved.

Hastily dragging on her jeans, plus two sweaters beneath the anorak of Barbara's she'd borrowed while helping with the snow clearing, Belinda froze into stillness as a new thought suddenly struck her. She knew . . . knew without a shadow of doubt, where her sister had gone.

Chapter Nine

Belinda's mind spun in wild confusion as the full significance of the situation reached her. It was only too glaringly evident now that Barbara was at Dorian Pettifer's cottage, trapped there by the return of the blizzard. Her sister would have thought it a great lark to ride over to see him by moonlight in the middle of the night while her husband and everyone else at Glyn-y-Fflur were all sound asleep. Possibly it had been a spur-of-the-moment decision, or more likely it had been planned when she was at Dorian's cottage in the afternoon. Belinda recalled her sister's obvious dismay at dinner when Adam had mentioned the forecast of another snowfall. Seeing the clear sky and moonlight, though, Barbara must have decided that the weathermen were wrong.

With an absolute conviction that she was right, Belinda agonized over what she ought to do. She'd had her fill of interfering between Adam and her sister and the temptation was terribly strong to take the view that this was *their* business, not hers, and leave well alone.

And yet . . . how could she do nothing? This wasn't a simple case of marital infidelity. A major search for Barbara was at this moment being put in hand by Adam; the men on the stud farm were being rounded up, to be sent off in different directions. One of them would attempt to get through to the outside world to alert the emergency services. In blizzard conditions such as this, lives might even be put at risk. Especially, she thought with an agonizing gasp, Adam's own life. She simply could not allow all that to be set in motion, all the inevitable risks taken, when she possessed the knowledge—or at least the certain conviction—that would render them unnecessary. Just as she was, her hair still tumbled from bed, she left the room and ran downstairs.

Adam and Huw were in the hall, with several of the men gathered round them. Belinda pushed her way through them, saying urgently, "Adam, I must speak to you."

"Have you got an idea about Barbie?" he asked, hope kindling in his dark eyes.

"Yes," she said. "I want to speak to you in private."

"But it's best for everyone to hear what you've got to say. We mustn't waste any time, Belinda. Weather conditions are deteriorating all the time and the longer we leave it the greater the risk that—"

"I need to talk to you *in private*," she repeated stubbornly. "Please, Adam!"

"Oh, very well." He turned to the men apologetically. "Hang on for a couple of minutes, will you?" Adam gestured her into his study, closing the door and limping over to her. "Well, out with it, Belinda. And for heaven's sake, hurry up!"

Faced with the moment of truth, she found it harder to tell him than she had imagined it would be. She took a deep breath and began. "Adam, I think I know where Barbara is. In fact, I'm certain of it. I believe that . . ." Her throat was tight and she had to swallow to try and clear away the constriction. In his impatience Adam took hold of her shoulders in a harsh grip, his fingers digging into her flesh while his stick dropped to the floor.

"Please, Belinda, tell me!"

"She . . . well, I don't think there can be any doubt that she's at Tyfawr, Dorian Pettifer's cottage."

Adam stared at her, bewildered. "What are you talking about? Why should Barbie be there?"

Merciful heaven, she thought, why do I have to go through with this? Telling tales about her sister was bad enough, but the pain she would be causing Adam made it ten times worse. If only there were some alternative!

"She . . . she's been seeing Dorian." It came out as a husky whisper.

"Seeing him?" Adam frowned, not understanding; then all at once his bewilderment vanished and he flared, "Are you suggesting that they've been having an affair?"

Belinda nodded in silence, her voice frozen in her throat by the savage intensity of his dark gaze. She knew instinctively that all his anger would be turned on her, not Barbara.

"You're lying!" he raged, his fingers digging even more cruelly into her shoulders. "Just because of some nasty little idea of getting even with Barbie! You're making up this whole ridiculous story. Admit it!"

"Please, Adam . . . you're hurting me."

"I'll hurt you a damn sight more before I'm through with you," he snarled. "Haven't you done enough harm to Barbie and me already without descending to this?"

"It . . . it's easy enough to check out whether I'm lying," she faltered unhappily. "If Barbie's *not* there, then . . ."

Adam stared at her for a long moment, then his arms fell away from her shoulders and he stepped back. "You really believe this, don't you?" he asked in a strained voice.

"Why else would I say it if I didn't? What good would it do me, Adam, to tell you a pack of lies that would soon be disproved?"

Breathing heavily, Adam pressed a hand against his head, trying to think. "How come you know about this, Belinda?"

"From Dorian himself," she admitted. "Like you, he mistook me for Barbara, and he insisted that I go to his cottage. He actually threatened to tell you about the . . . the relationship, if I didn't."

"You mean to say that you actually went?" Then, before Belinda could form any words of explanation, he added harshly, "I suppose I shouldn't be surprised, though, knowing the sort of person you are."

"But I only went in order to finish his relationship with Barbara," she protested in a broken voice. "I thought . . . if I could see Dorian, as Barbara, and make him understand that everything was finished between them . . . well, you need never have discovered the truth."

"Another of your charming little deceptions!"

"I did it for the best, Adam," she pleaded desperately. "It seemed to me that if I could manage to square things with Dorian, then at least you would be spared that much additional pain."

His jaw was still set against her and there was no relenting of his dreadful anger. "When was it you went to Pettifer's cottage, Belinda?"

"The day before yesterday, in the afternoon. I'd

just returned when you met me in the hall and told me about getting the phone call from Barbara."

"So you could have told me about it then, for heaven's sake!"

"But with Barbara coming back to you there was all the more reason *not* to tell you, Adam. At least, that was the way it seemed to me at the time. You were badly shaken and very bewildered . . . furious with me, yet ready to take Barbara back. It would have added a terrible complication to have revealed this affair with Dorian, too. And I honestly thought that it was all over. He'd agreed, you see, not to use any more threats or anything, but just to let the relationship die."

"Yet, even so, you still insist that Barbie must be with him now?"

She lowered her eyes from his bitterly accusing gaze. "Yes, I do."

"What makes you so certain that Barbie went to see him?"

Belinda clenched her fists. Why was it necessary for him to go through this prolonged torture? But once launched, there was no holding back. She had to tell Adam everything she knew about her sister's sordid liaison. "Barbie and I had a talk about Dorian Pettifer and she told me straight out that she intended to see him again. I explained to her, you see, about having gone to see him myself. I thought it would set her mind at rest, now that you two were making an entirely fresh start, to know that her foolish affair with him was decently buried and could be forgotten."

"Yet despite what you told her, Barbie insisted on going to see him?"

Belinda nodded wretchedly. "I pleaded with her, but she wouldn't listen. She rode over there yesterday afternoon. Afterward when I went up to her room to try to get her to come down and massage your shoulders, she told me so."

Adam's face was drawn and taut, drained of all color. When he spoke, his voice was hoarse and scarcely above a murmur. "Go on, Belinda. Tell me the rest of what you know."

"There isn't anything more . . . nothing definite. Just guesswork. Barbara was in a curious mood last evening at dinner—you must have noticed it yourself. I should have realized that something was in the wind, some crazy stunt like going to see Dorian again during the night."

Adam stood utterly still and rigid, as if stunned beyond words by this revelation. Belinda felt quite scared by the expression in his eyes and went on beseechingly, "I dreaded having to tell you. . . . I knew what a shock it would be, but you must see that I had no choice. How could I allow people to risk their lives on a fruitless search for Barbie when I knew all along exactly where she must be?"

Adam didn't answer. He regarded Belinda distantly, as if she were a stranger to him.

"Please," she begged, "don't look at me like that. Everything I've done was meant for the best. Only it's all gone so horribly wrong. . . ."

He nodded vaguely, but Belinda couldn't be sure that he had really heard her. "I'll have to get over there right away," he muttered.

"What do you mean?" she gasped, appalled.

"To the cottage. I'll have to go there."

"But you *can't,* Adam! Not all that way and with the weather like this."

"I've *got* to go," he said again. "How can I possibly send another man to find my errant wife?"

"I'll go instead," Belinda volunteered wildly.

"Even less could I allow *you* to go. This is a job that I have to do myself."

"But in your condition you might . . . you might get killed, Adam."

A grim, fleeting smile came and vanished. "I won't do that. I'm too old a hand on this terrain. I've seen blizzards before."

"But . . . couldn't you telephone?"

"I've told you, all the lines are down."

Belinda's thoughts raced frantically. She knew, with terrifying certainty, that there was no stopping Adam. And he wasn't prepared to take another man along as witness to his shame. She said quickly, with pressing insistence, "I'm coming with you, then."

"You can't," he said, jerking.

"I can and I will. You can't stop me."

"Don't be a fool, Belinda," he said distractedly. "Haven't I got enough problems, without you—"

"You're only wasting time," she pointed out. "I take it you're not considering riding?"

"No chance, in this weather. I'll use skis. Which is another reason," he added, "why you can't come with me."

"I can ski," she flashed. "You taught me, remember?"

"But you haven't any skis."

"Barbara has, though. She told me so."

For a moment she thought Adam would still argue. Then he accepted defeat. "Very well, Belinda. You'll find her ski suit in one of the closets in our bedroom. Mine, too, so throw it down to me. I'll get the skis out."

The group of men waiting in the hall stared at them curiously as she and Adam emerged from the study. Belinda went straight past them and ran up the stairs, leaving all the explanations to him. What Adam told them she didn't know, but when she descended again, wearing the bright yellow parka and black pants, the hall was empty. As she waited, tense and nervous, Megan came hurrying from the kitchen carrying a knapsack.

"Oh, Miss Vaughn," she burst out worriedly, "why has Adam called off the search? My Dai would gladly go, and Huw and the others. Adam shouldn't set foot outside in this awful weather, not the way he is. And you . . . well, you're only a slip of a girl and you don't know this country at all."

At that moment Adam emerged from his study, clad in the blue ski suit that Belinda had thrown down to him, and she was saved from having to invent a plausible explanation.

"Ah, good, Megan, some hot coffee and food for us. Thanks a lot."

Taking the knapsack, Adam turned at once to the front door, where the two pairs of skis were propped against the wall. He and Belinda carried them outside and put them on in the partial shelter of the portico. Watching him covertly, Belinda saw that even bending to do this comparatively simple action caused him pain. She knew that it was sheer lunacy for him to set out on such an expedition, yet there was nothing she could do to prevent it. As the two of them started off they encountered the full fury of the blizzard. Fearfully Belinda wondered what lay ahead of them.

Adam halted as he had done a number of times before to ease his cramped muscles. Belinda guessed that behind the concealing parka hood and goggles his face would be a mask of pain. Twice she had suggested turning back while there was still time and twice Adam had flatly refused.

They were still on the lower slopes of the valley's flank, but by now the rise was steep enough to necessitate taking a zigzag course and soon it would become steeper still, reducing their progress to a mere crawl. They hardly spoke to each other; it was an effort above the howling of the wind and they needed to conserve their energy.

All around them was a whirling whiteness and it was impossible to see anything more than about ten yards ahead. This was the route Barbara must have taken, but Belinda had long since given up searching the ground for any telltale signs. Keffel's hoofprints would long ago have been obliterated by the snow that had fallen since.

For the last part of the climb they were obliged to take sideways steps and every yard of height they gained seemed to Belinda like a major victory. Once, the skis shot from under her and she fell awkwardly onto her side. At once Adam was bending over her anxiously.

"Belinda, are you okay?" he shouted.

"Yes," she gasped breathlessly. "Just help me up, will you?"

Standing, he didn't relinquish his hold on her at once. Even through the thick quilting of her ski suit Belinda was acutely aware of his grip on her arm. Just for a few seconds there was an electrifying tension between them again; then, self-consciously, Adam let go and stood back.

"We'd better press on."

The final stretch before they reached the hill crest took another half-hour of fighting all the way. And once at the top the wind struck them with fresh ferocity. But at least, with the terrain stretching ahead in a series of undulations, progress would be a little easier now. Together they skied down the first slope and the impetus took them halfway up the next rise. Then again, down and up, and yet again. At long last Belinda glimpsed the vague shape of the little farm cottage through the whirling snow. As they skied down toward it she realized with a clutch of fear that there was no sign of smoke rising from the squat chimney.

Had she, after all, made a terrible mistake? Had she cruelly misjudged her sister and condemned Adam to this nightmare trek for nothing? Worse still, had she by her intervention called off the search that might have saved Barbara's life? The significance of there being no smoke didn't seem to have struck Adam. He was pressing on to the door which, since it was on the sheltered side, was luckily not blocked by a snowdrift. Stopping only to unclip his skis, he banged on the door with his fist.

There was no response from within.

Adam banged again, then shouted, but to no effect. He took hold of the handle to shake it and to their surprise the door sprang open. They stumbled inside, thankful to have gained shelter at last from the howling blizzard. The living room had a lingering warmth, but the stove had burned out.

With a sudden decision Belinda darted to the staircase and ran up to the bedroom above. If Barbie and Dorian *were* up there it was better that she, not Adam, should find them. But the bedroom was empty, the bed made, though carelessly. In a daze of disbelief that she should have been wrong Belinda went slowly downstairs again.

Adam was standing by the table, a sheet of notepaper in his hand. Even from across the room she recognized Barbie's large, sprawly handwriting.

"What does it say?" she asked, not knowing whether to be fearful or relieved.

With a hopeless gesture he handed her the letter. "You were right, Belinda," he muttered hoarsely. "Even more right than you guessed!"

Adam,
    By the time this gets into your hands I'll be out of your life for good. Now that the snow has

started again it's obvious that I'll never be able to ride back to Glyn-y-Fflur before morning and if I stay here everything will inevitably come out. So I'm off with Dorian while the track is still passable. We'll be going straight to London and staying at his flat. But don't come chasing after us, because this time it really is finished between you and me. I realized that coming back to Wales was a ghastly mistake almost from the first moment I arrived. You and I are too different ever to be able to make a go of things. I guess I should never have set out to pinch you from Belinda in Switzerland, because you two would really have been much better suited to each other. Don't be too hard on her for what she's done, Adam. I was mad at her myself at first, but not anymore. Knowing Bel as well as I do, I guess she did it for purely unselfish reasons. And the poor girl has never stopped being crazy about you!

Love and kisses,
Barbie

P.S. Keffel's safe in the shed at the back. We're leaving her plenty of hay and water, so she'll come to no harm.

Belinda looked at Adam, unable to find words to express her turbulent emotions. There was thankfulness that her sister was safe, yet a terrible anger against Barbie for doing this to Adam. He had pulled off his goggles and she saw with dismay how terribly gaunt he looked.

Impulsively she gripped his arm and urged him toward the sofa.

"You must rest, Adam," she said, easing off the knapsack that was still on his back. Unstrapping it, she took out the vacuum flask and the next moment she was holding out a mug of steaming coffee to him. "Here, drink this. It will buck you up."

Adam shook his head. "No, you first."

"Do as I say!" Suddenly she felt in charge of the situation. Adam was exhausted by the wearying journey, which only sheer willpower could have got him through, and on top of that he'd had a traumatic shock. For the moment he was deeply vulnerable and needed her strength. And she found, to her relieved amazement, that she had the strength to give him. After making him drink the hot coffee she went across to the stove. Opening up the dampers, heaping on kindling and then logs, she soon had it blazing warmly.

That done, she gave a thought to Keffel. Redonning her parka, she went to the outer door, saying, "I'll only be a few minutes."

Outside she plodded through blinding snow to the shed at the rear of the cottage. A drift against the door blocked access, but it had obviously been cleared away once and the shovel was propped nearby. Wielding this, Belinda soon moved enough snow to get the shed door open. She was relieved to find Keffel quite comfortable inside. As Barbara had said in her note, there was plenty of water and a broken-open bale of hay—no doubt purchased by Dorian to provide for Keffel during Barbara's visits. The pony whinnied with delight at seeing her and Belinda lingered a few moments, patting the mare's golden neck and talking to her softly. Then she said apologetically, "I must go now, Keffel. But you'll be just fine in here, won't you? I'll come back later on. That's a promise!"

When she reentered the cottage Adam asked anxiously, "Where have you been?"

"I was just checking to make sure that Keffel was safe and sound. She's okay."

"Thank heaven for that." He gave a deep sigh.

"Barbie has really gone for good this time, hasn't she?"

Belinda looked at him with pity in her heart. But there was a feeling of anger and bitterness, too, at the thought of all the wasted love and devotion Adam had poured out on her uncaring sister. If only that same love were bestowed upon herself, how she would treasure and nurture it!

Outside, the blizzard still raged. They were stuck here, she knew, and she voiced her concern that the people at Glyn-y-Fflur would be worried about their long absence.

Adam shook his head. "I told Huw not to expect us back until there's an improvement in the weather."

"How much did you explain to Huw?" she asked.

"As little as possible. He tried to insist on coming with me instead of you. But he seemed to understand that I couldn't allow that."

Huw was very shrewd, Belinda thought. Perhaps he'd guessed the truth about her sister's frequent excursions. It brought her a shred of comfort to know that Adam would have a loyal friend at hand in the difficult period that lay ahead while he came to terms with Barbara's desertion. With a sigh she shelved the problems that tomorrow would bring. For the time being they were safe and snug here. Apart from the food Megan had packed, there were supplies in the larder, Belinda found. She set to work fixing a meal, making a large omelet and toasting bread. And she persuaded Adam to take a glass of Dorian's whiskey, which brought a faint touch of color to his face.

After they'd eaten, Belinda made fresh coffee and sat with him before the glowing stove. There was a feeling of sympathy between them, all hostility gone.

And yet there existed, too, a barrier of restraint that kept them silent.

The wind seemed to be lessening in intensity. Belinda rose quietly and went to the window. It had almost stopped snowing, she saw, and although the winter day was wearing on, there was a little more light in the sky. Would it be possible, she wondered, for them to return to Glyn-y-Fflur this afternoon? Without the driving snow to face, and with the way mostly downhill, it would be less arduous than the outward journey had been.

She turned round to ask Adam what he thought, then dismissed the idea at once. Exhaustion had overcome him and he was lying back against the sofa cushions with his eyes closed, obviously asleep. And in sleep, though the lines of pain were absent from his features, he looked intensely vulnerable, so that her heart turned over in pity and love. Very gently she made his head more comfortable. A lock of dark hair fell across his brow and she drew it back with one fingertip. Then she sat down beside him, watching his face, and fell into a poignant reverie of what might have been.

An hour passed and the daylight began to fade. The blizzard was spent and beyond the occasional stirring of a log in the stove everything was silent. And then, breaking into the stillness, came Adam's voice, startling her, for in the darkening room she hadn't realized that he had wakened.

"How can I ever apologize to you, Belinda," he murmured huskily, "for the way I've misjudged you all along the line?"

"You don't have to apologize," she said in a low tone, tears springing to her eyes. "It was understandable, considering. I feel terrible about what's happened, Adam. Barbara is my sister, my twin, and I can't help feeling a certain respon-

sibility for what she's done. The way she's behaved."

"But you mustn't! How can you be responsible for
Barbie's actions?" Adam pushed himself upright and
reached for her hand, gripping it tightly. "It's bewildering to me that two sisters can look so exactly alike
and yet be so utterly different in character. I've
been such a fool, Belinda. A complete and utter
fool!"

"You couldn't have known . . ."

"I should at least have realized," he cut across her
in bitter self-reproach, "that those things Barbie said
about you in Switzerland couldn't possibly be
true . . . about you being more or less engaged to
a chap back home in New York, that you were just
amusing yourself by pretending to be serious about
me. That was all just something she invented,
wasn't it, to break things up between us?"

"Yes," Belinda whispered shakily. "Cliff Willis
was a co-worker and we'd dated a couple of times.
Barbie knew perfectly well that there was never
anything serious between Cliff and me."

Adam's eyes on her face were steady. "When you
introduced me to Barbie I was deceived by the
uncanny physical resemblance. In my mind I en-
dowed her with the same qualities that I'd seen in
you. You two seemed to me wonderful beyond
imagination. Looking back now, I can't understand
how it was that I started to see more of Barbie than
of you . . . but that's the way it happened. And then
when she told me all those things about you—with a
great show of reluctance—oh, how could I have
been so stupid? And ever since, Belinda, ever since
Barbie and I were married, I've shut my eyes to the
increasingly obvious truth. I just couldn't face admitting to myself that I'd made such a ghastly
blunder."

It was an agony to Belinda to sit there with her hand in his. She knew that if Adam made the slightest move toward her she would be in his arms in an instant. With an effort she pulled her hand away and stood up, making a pretense that the stove needed replenishing.

From behind her Adam asked in a low, intense voice, "What Barbie said in her letter—about the way you've always felt about me—Belinda, is *that* true?"

Belinda stood with her back still to him, frozen into stillness. What could she say? Confess that she loved him . . . desperately, hopelessly? That she'd been in love with him almost from the day they met and would continue to love him until the day she died? She clenched her fists, feeling something that was almost anger against Adam for demanding so much of her.

"Yes, it's true," she whispered at last.

Adam gave a low groan of misery. "So I've ruined your life as well as mine by my crass stupidity. I'm sorry, Belinda, so dreadfully sorry. That seems a pitifully inadequate thing to say, but what else *can* I say?"

There was no answer to that and the fleeting seconds stretched into an eternity. And then, when the tension seemed beyond bearing, a sound from outside penetrated the stillness in the room. The sound, surely, of a vehicle? Belinda and Adam stared at each other questioningly for a moment. Then he rose painfully to his feet and they both went to the window. From out of the gray dusk headlights flashed dazzlingly on the snow. A dark shape lurched into view—a truck of some kind, which slithered to a stop outside. In the sudden return of silence as the engine was shut off a cheerful voice boomed, "Anyone home?"

Belinda dashed to the door and dragged it open. "Oh, it's good to see you!" she cried to the man muffled up in a sheepskin jacket who was stomping through the thick snow toward her. "We didn't think that anyone would be able to get through."

"The track's passable, just about, with four-wheel drive and chains," he said. Then, looking puzzled, he exclaimed, "Why, it's Mrs. Lloyd! And Adam! I was expecting to find that TV writer chap all on his own here—and probably more than a bit scared of being snowbound."

"Dorian isn't here, Ivor," explained Adam. "And this isn't my wife, it's her twin sister, Belinda Vaughn. Belinda, meet Ivor Rhys."

"Well, I'll be!" The man pulled off his woolly cap and scratched his head in perplexity. "How come you're here, Adam? I heard you were hurt in a fall."

Adam stood to one side to let him in. "It's a long story," he said, "and you'll be wanting to get away. We've got a mare here in the shed at the back, too."

Ivor Rhys looked in bewilderment from one to the other, but tactfully decided not to ask any more questions for the time being. "No problem," he said. "The mare can follow behind in our tracks. So let's get going before it decides to start snowing again."

Chapter Ten

On a Saturday afternoon of blazing July heat Belinda watched the by-now-familiar scenery unwinding outside the train windows. She loved each and every one of the mountain peaks that were etched against the vividly blue sky, each wooded valley and rushing stream, each nestling village and isolated mountain.

After rattling through the last short tunnel the local train rumbled over a small stone bridge and with what seemed to Belinda like a hoot of joy drew up at the little wayside station. Clutching her luggage, she threw open the door and jumped down into Adam's waiting arms.

"Darling," he exclaimed, holding her and the luggage all bundled up together and kissing her with practiced thoroughness. "Is it really only a fortnight since I last saw you in London?"

Belinda laughed happily. "Did it seem longer?"

"Like a lifetime!" He kissed her again, then with arms entwined they walked to his waiting car. Soon they were speeding along the narrow country lanes beneath arching tunnels of lush summer foliage and finally climbing the pass that led into Glyn-y-Fflur. Adam drew to a halt at the highest point, where the valley lay spread before them. Belinda had seen it snowbound in winter, then brilliant with a spring carpeting of the wild flowers, which gave the valley its name. Now, in high summer, a shimmering heat haze rose from the paddocks where the mares grazed peacefully with their frisky foals.

For a few moments the two of them sat very still, looking down at the lovely scene. Then Adam turned to her and they came together in a long, passionate kiss.

"Oh, Belinda, darling." He sighed as he drew back. "It seems almost too good to be true that in less than a week's time we shall be married."

To Belinda too it seemed like a miracle, for there had been so much sorrow and suffering along the way to their happiness. For a while, after Barbara's tragic death in the blizzard, she and Adam had been stunned with shock. The news of the accident had reached them soon after they, and Keffel, were safely returned to Glyn-y-Fflur, the pass having been cleared by a snowplow and the phone lines restored. It emerged that, in the rapidly worsening weather conditions, Dorian Pettifer's car had skidded out of control while turning on the open mountain road and plunged an almost vertical two hundred feet.

"What those two thought they were doing, on that stretch of road in such weather, it's difficult to fathom," said the police officer who came to break the news. "They didn't stand a chance, poor things!"

Immediately after the funeral Belinda had returned to her job in London. Though Adam talked of keeping in touch, after all the anguish he'd suffered she doubted if he'd want further contact with his wife's twin sister, who would only serve to remind him of the unhappy past. So it was a great joy when, three evenings later, her home phone rang and it was Adam.

"How are you, Belinda?" he'd asked.

"Me? Oh, I'm okay, Adam. What about you, though?"

"Making good progress. Another week and I'll be riding again."

"Don't rush things," she cautioned anxiously.

It was the first of many phone calls from Adam. And then toward the end of March he had announced that he was coming to London. "I need a break, but I'm afraid it can't be for more than one night at this time of year, with the foaling about to start."

Though his visit delighted Belinda there was a reticence in both of them. Their conversation was guarded and they kept to generalities. Adam, seeming his old fit self again, took her to the theater, and then out for a late supper. After driving her back to her flat in Chelsea he didn't attempt to come in.

"I was wondering," he said tentatively. "Would you feel like coming to Glyn-y-Fflur for Easter?"

Belinda's heart expanded at the thought, but she said doubtfully, "Would it be wise, Adam? Everybody must know the whole story by now."

"If it would embarrass you . . ." he began, disappointment in his voice.

"But it was you I was thinking of," she said quickly.

"Then don't worry about it, Belinda." He leaned over and kissed her on the cheek. "Please come."

Belinda was terribly apprehensive that first time, but as it turned out, she need not have been. Whatever the staff of the stud farm thought, they kept their opinions to themselves and she received a warm and friendly welcome. Huw greeted her with a certain wistfulness, but she knew that he had long since abandoned any hopes in her direction.

Belinda went to Glyn-y-Fflur again in June, for a slightly longer stay this time. After dinner on the first evening, when Megan had cleared away and departed, she and Adam sat together on the veranda watching the colors fade from the valley and melt into the deepening shadows. As the dusk gathered more closely around them they fell silent. At last Adam began to speak in a low, hesitant voice.

"You remember, Belinda, what I said to you when we were snowbound at Dorian Pettifer's cottage? About not being able to face the fact that I'd made a terrible mistake in asking Barbie to marry me instead of you? It's quite true, you know. Right from the very start I was living in a world of pretense, trying to convince myself that I was happy. Despite all the evidence that our marriage wasn't working out I kept insisting to myself that I was passionately in love with Barbie and that everything was going to come out right for us. And then that January afternoon when you walked into my hospital room I felt overjoyed, because I sensed at once that here was what I'd been seeking ever since my wedding day: the sweetness and gentleness and concern for me that I longed to believe were characteristic of the woman I'd chosen to marry. I fell in love all over again in those fateful days, Belinda, and I felt wonderfully happy and confident about the future. So you can imagine my anger and confusion when I discovered that you weren't my wife at all."

"Poor Barbie," said Belinda with a heavy sigh. "She must have been a very unhappy person deep down. Once she got whatever it was she wanted, she stopped wanting it and yearned for something else instead. It was the same all her life."

Adam glanced at her with a sort of wonder. "You're very generous, Belinda. You find it so easy to forgive her for what she did to you."

"Not easy," she said candidly. "But there's a special tug of affinity between identical twins that nothing can ever quite destroy. Barbie often made me furious . . . resentful . . . jealous. But those feelings never persisted for long. We somehow belonged to each other—and we always would have, come what may."

"What about me?" Adam asked softly. "Can you find it in you to forgive me, too?"

"I forgave you, for everything, a long time ago," she murmured.

Slowly, as if in a floating dream, Adam gathered her into his arms and kissed her long and deep. It was the first kiss of passion they had exchanged in all these months and Belinda felt breathless and elated when he finally let her go.

"Oh, Belinda, I love you so much," he said, his voice shaky with emotion.

"And I love you, Adam."

"I want us to be married," he said huskily. "I only wish it could be at once. Tomorrow."

Belinda couldn't resist a gentle tease. "You seem very sure that I'll say yes."

In the darkness she heard him catch his breath. "If you felt that you'd never be able to settle in Glyn-y-Fflur I'd understand. I could sell up here and we'd find another place. Maybe that would be best. . . ."

"No, Adam," she said quickly, decidedly. "Don't even think of it. Glyn-y-Fflur means too much to you to throw it all away."

"But your happiness is infinitely more important to me, Belinda darling."

"My happiness," she said steadily, "is being with you. Of course I'll marry you, Adam, and this is where we shall live."

"If you're quite sure?"

"Quite, quite sure!"

They kissed again and Belinda gloried in the feeling of his strong arms about her. To look at Adam these days, it seemed incredible to remember that this bronzed, virile, superbly muscled man had only a few short months ago been an invalid.

The moon had risen above the mountaintops and its pure, clear, shimmering light seemed to be an omen for their future together. As she and Adam happily made their plans the sweet, silver voice of a nightingale floated to them on the fragrant evening air and a pony in one of the paddocks whinnied as if in response.

That Saturday evening in July Huw and Elspeth were coming to dinner. Belinda had learned with great delight that a romance was blooming between Adam's stud groom and the hospital physiotherapist. She wondered if she herself had played a part in bringing them together by pointing Huw in the right direction. She liked to think so, because she felt a deep sense of affection and gratitude toward Huw and she wanted him to find happiness.

Elspeth had apparently been spending the afternoon with Huw and his grandmother, but soon after seven they strolled across to the big house. Elspeth was looking very pretty in a flowery blue summer dress and they both seemed a little flushed to Belinda. The reason emerged over predinner drinks on the veranda.

"We've got something to tell you," Huw began and dried up, suddenly tongue-tied.

"Like you've fixed the day?" Adam suggested with a grin.

"You've guessed!"

"Not a very difficult thing to do when you two are obviously crazy about each other."

"Look who's talking!" retorted Huw.

They all laughed and Adam asked, "Well, when's it to be?"

"We want to make it October, if that's okay with you, Adam? Things will be fairly quiet here then and Elspeth fancies going somewhere in the sun for a couple of weeks. Spain, maybe."

"Great! But no looking at horses, mind!"

Huw chuckled. "I doubt if I'll have the time!"

The atmosphere was suddenly lighthearted. Half an hour later they sat down to Megan's beef-and-mushroom casserole with keen appetites. But Belinda had hardly started to serve before there was an interruption, Megan hurrying in to say that her husband, Dai, wanted to see Adam urgently.

"Right, Megan. Fetch Dai in, will you?"

He appeared in the doorway, looking apologetic. "A pity it is to disturb you, Adam, but Rowella's filly has had an accident. Tried to jump the fence, I reckon, silly young idiot. And now she's got a cut knee."

Adam and Huw were on their feet immediately. "Sorry about breaking up the party," said Adam with a rueful smile. "You two ladies go ahead and have your dinner. We'll try not to be too long."

As the three men went out together Belinda looked across at Elspeth. "I don't know how you feel, but I'm for going after them."

"You bet!"

Belinda turned to Megan. "You wouldn't mind putting your casserole back in the oven for a bit?"

Megan nodded cheerfully. "It'll come to no great harm. Off you go."

Belinda and Elspeth caught up with the men at Huw's office, where they had collected the first-aid box. As they jumped into the Land Rover that was parked outside Belinda shouted, "Hey, wait for us!"

"There was no need for you to spoil your meal," said Adam from behind the wheel as they ran up.

"But we want to come," she told him, and Elspeth nodded firmly.

He smiled in warm approval. "Jump in, then."

Adam drove quickly along the sandy track between the paddock fences to one at the far end of the valley. There they found young Davy anxiously waiting beside a beautiful little chestnut filly and its dam, trying to keep them calm. While Adam and Huw gave their attention to the filly Belinda went to the agitated mare, talking to her softly and holding her halter firmly to keep her from interfering.

The injury, Adam announced at once, wasn't too serious, not bad enough to need calling in the vet. Belinda watched as he and Huw between them deftly washed the wounded knee, clipped away some of the surrounding hair, then dusted it with an antibiotic powder and bound it lightly with lint. Finally Adam gave the timid little creature an anti-tetanus injection.

"There, baby!" he said, patting her affectionately on the rump. "You'll be okay now. And a lesson learned, I hope . . . those fences are not for jumping!"

Within just a few minutes the foal was already nibbling the sweet grass again, all the alarm and excitement forgotten. Adam looked on in rueful amusement.

"The little demon is quite unrepentant about ruining our dinner party," he said laughingly. "But I'm afraid that's the way it is on a stud farm. And this is nothing to what it's like at foaling time. We're lucky to get an unbroken night's sleep then. Mares always seem to choose the early hours to give birth."

"I guess we'll survive," said Belinda. "Check, Elspeth?"

"Check!" the other girl responded, her eyes fondly on Huw.

Their belated meal was a cheerful occasion. It was going to be the forerunner of many such dinner parties, Belinda knew . . . two young married couples, four good friends.

Later Belinda and Adam stood on the front steps watching the other pair strolling back to Huw's bungalow, where Elspeth had left her car.

"Those two are going to be very happy," said Belinda as they went back inside.

"Aren't we, too?" teased Adam.

She turned to him and slid her arms up about his neck. "Oh, yes, darling, so blissfully happy. Always and always!"

Their kiss was deeply passionate and lingering, carrying Belinda to heady peaks of sensual awareness and giving her tantalizing glimpses of the ecstasy that was to come. At length Adam pushed her away from him with a regretful sigh.

"Off with you to your lonely bed, temptress, or I won't answer for the consequences. Thank heaven that in four days' time I shan't need to say good night to you ever again."

IT'S YOUR OWN SPECIAL TIME

Contemporary romances for today's women.
Each month, six very special love stories will be yours
from SILHOUETTE. Look for them wherever books are sold
or order now from the coupon below.

$1.50 each

Hampson	☐ 1 ☐ 4 ☐ 16 ☐ 27 ☐ 28 ☐ 52 ☐ 94	Browning	☐ 12 ☐ 38 ☐ 53 ☐ 73 ☐ 93
Stanford	☐ 6 ☐ 25 ☐ 35 ☐ 46 ☐ 58 ☐ 88	Michaels	☐ 15 ☐ 32 ☐ 61 ☐ 87
		John	☐ 17 ☐ 34 ☐ 57 ☐ 85
Hastings	☐ 13 ☐ 26	Beckman	☐ 8 ☐ 37 ☐ 54 ☐ 96
Vitek	☐ 33 ☐ 47 ☐ 84	Wisdom	☐ 49 ☐ 95
Wildman	☐ 29 ☐ 48	Halston	☐ 62 ☐ 83

☐ 5 Goforth
☐ 7 Lewis
☐ 9 Wilson
☐ 10 Caine
☐ 11 Vernon
☐ 14 Oliver
☐ 19 Thornton
☐ 20 Fulford
☐ 21 Richards

☐ 22 Stephens
☐ 23 Edwards
☐ 24 Healy
☐ 30 Dixon
☐ 31 Halldorson
☐ 36 McKay
☐ 39 Sinclair
☐ 43 Robb
☐ 45 Carroll

☐ 50 Scott
☐ 55 Ladame
☐ 56 Trent
☐ 59 Vernon
☐ 60 Hill
☐ 63 Brent
☐ 71 Ripy
☐ 76 Hardy
☐ 78 Oliver

☐ 81 Roberts
☐ 82 Dailey
☐ 86 Adams
☐ 89 James
☐ 90 Major
☐ 92 McKay
☐ 97 Clay
☐ 98 St. George
☐ 99 Camp

$1.75 each

Stanford	☐ 100 ☐ 112 ☐ 131	Browning	☐ 113 ☐ 142 ☐ 164 ☐ 172
Hardy	☐ 101 ☐ 130	Michaels	☐ 114 ☐ 146
Cork	☐ 103 ☐ 148	Beckman	☐ 124 ☐ 154 ☐ 179
Vitek	☐ 104 ☐ 139 ☐ 157 ☐ 176	Roberts	☐ 127 ☐ 143 ☐ 163 ☐ 180
Dailey	☐ 106 ☐ 118 ☐ 153 ☐ 177	Trent	☐ 110 ☐ 161
Bright	☐ 107 ☐ 125	Wisdom	☐ 132 ☐ 166
Hampson	☐ 108 ☐ 119 ☐ 128 ☐ 136 ☐ 147 ☐ 151 ☐ 155 ☐ 160 ☐ 178	Hunter	☐ 137 ☐ 167
		Scott	☐ 117 ☐ 169
		Sinclair	☐ 123 ☐ 174

$1.75 each

Silhouette Desire
15-Day Trial Offer
A new romance series
that explores
contemporary relationships
in exciting detail

Six Silhouette Desire romances, free for 15 days!
We'll send you six new Silhouette Desire romances
to look over for 15 days, absolutely free! If you decide
not to keep the books, return them and owe nothing.

Six books a month, free home delivery. If you like
Silhouette Desire romances as much as we think you
will, keep them and return your payment with the
invoice. Then we will send you six new books every
month to preview, just as soon as they are published.
You pay only for the books you decide to keep, and
you never pay postage and handling.

Silhouette Romance

Coming next month from
Silhouette Romances

When Love Comes by Anne Hampson

Janis was perfectly content with being single until Clive Trent stepped into her life. But their happiness was threatened by Madame de Vivonne and the secret in Janis' past.

Season of Enchantment by Ashley Summers

The accident that introduced Christina Lacey to Daniel Belmont was a blessing in disguise. He offered her a challenging new job — and challenges that had nothing to do with business.

London Pride by Elizabeth Hunter

Joanne Rodgers, a well brought-up parson's daughter met her match when playboy barrister William Oliver decided to enlist her to help him advance her career!

From This Day by Nora Roberts

B.J. Clark, manager of the Lakeside Inn, was prepared to dislike Taylor Reynolds, the new owner and renovater. What she wasn't prepared for was the devastating passion he aroused in her.

Savage Moon by Frances Lloyd

Determined to find her only living relative, Laura Fairchild set forth across the wilderness of central Australia with rugged rancher "Mac" MacDougall, the only man who could take her there.

Tears Of Gold by Cynthia Starr

Vacationing in Peru, Angela Jorgen unsuspectingly fell in with her sister's plans — pretending she was the fianceé of Raoul del Rey. The pretense became reality when Raoul insisted on their marriage.